# Vengeance is Mine

# Leon opio

IG
Indie Gypsy
PO Box 511002
Livonia, MI 48151
http://www.indiegypsy.com

©2014 by Leon Opio
Cover Design - Indie Gypsy
ISBN-10: 0615990142
ISBN-13: 978-0615990149
LCCN: 2014942404

For information on special discounts on paperback edition contact us at orders@indiegypsy.com.

# Acknowledgments

I want to give thanks to the staff at Indie Gypsy Publishing for all the help they have given me in making my book come to life. The new book cover, promotional material and book trailer has really taken my vision and made it into a reality.

# DEDICATIONS

I wanted to thank God for the blessing he gives me every day.

I also want to thank my wife Tabitha for her love, support and encouragement during my writing journey and both my daughters Alexis and Arlene for their encouragement and support.

# CHAPTER 1

These empty streets haven't seen life in years. The only sign of movement is the debris coming together like a mini tornado from the warm night air blowing briskly. The few structures that still stand are abandoned storefronts; an eye sore in an area that has seen better times. Among the remaining buildings in this dilapidated neighborhood, the one that stands out is a large structure that provided the majority of the jobs for the area.

Wilson Lumber employed over three hundred employees before closing over ten years ago. There were many theories on why the mill closed, but once people began losing their jobs, other businesses in the area slowly began to follow suit. This once bustling small neighborhood became a modern ghost town as families who had lived here for years lost their homes. Many left to seek work elsewhere and make a new life for themselves. But sometimes to find closure in one's life, one must go back to the beginning. Tonight is no exception as a small private gathering is being held at the mill for that exact purpose.

A scream resonates through the silence of a cold, dark, damp room. A bed is visible in the far corner of the room, bolted to a dirty, stained concrete floor. A lone dimly lit light bulb hangs from the ceiling giving off a faint glow in the windowless space.

Lying on the bed is a woman who appears to be in her mid-40's, wearing a tight fitting, low-cut blouse and short skirt, which may have been worn to impress someone, but now they are just dirty, stained and wrinkled. Her hair hangs disheveled in front of her face and is in dire need of a comb. She raises her head, opening her eyes slowly trying to adjust to the dim lighting in the room.

She scans the room, sees nothing but a steel door with no knob and a small sliding door at the bottom of it. She notices that the walls in the room are made of brick and as she continues looking around the room, she realizes that the room is windowless.

She cautiously sits up, swings her legs off the bed and places her feet on the floor. When her feet touch the floor, the cool sensation on her feet make her look down and she realizes that her shoes are missing.

At that exact moment she also notices there is something attached to her left ankle; a large metal shackle. She lifts her left leg to find there is a large rusty chain attached to the shackle which is also chained to the rear leg of the bed that is bolted to the floor.

Her mind begins to race, putting her in a panic and her breathing accelerates as she looks down rubbing her eyes, hoping it's just her mind playing tricks on her. After a few seconds, she raises her head hoping that her delusion has passed, but when her eyes open the realization that this is not a dream or a delusion dawns on her.

Instantly, she attempts to slip the shackle off her ankle. She halts upon feeling her skin roughly tearing and begins to see blood trickling down toward the heel of her foot.

Giving up on the restraint, she begins to furiously tug at the chain, praying she has the strength to rip it from its holder. It doesn't budge. Her emotions pour out, going from fear to frenzy and settling into terror as she screams, while still viciously pulling at the chain.

"Help me! Please! Can anybody hear me?!"

She continues yelling with the hope that someone will hear her pleas, but after what seems like an eternity, she hears no response to her screams. She looks around the room in fear, wondering if there was something, anything that she could find that would help.

Sadly, the flickering light bulb hanging from the ceiling appear to be the only thing is this room that is not bolted down, which can't help her, so she reverts to shouting once again.

"Is anybody out there?! Please, someone help me! Anybody!"

Once again, all she hears are the echoes of her own screams. She punches the bed in frustration.

"Damn it! Please, someone help me!"

She slides down to the floor and leans her head weakly against the bed, feeling completely helpless; not knowing how she got here and fearing that no one is coming to her aid. In the midst of her sobs a noise from outside the steel door causes her to raise her head. The noise gives her a ray of hope that someone may have heard her and is coming to save her.

"Hello! Is anybody there? I'm in here!"

The noise is coming from the bottom of the door, when the small sliding door opens; a gloved hand pushes in two silver bowls on a tray. She stands proceeding toward the entrance quickly as possible, but in her weaken state the chain cause's her body to slam to the ground. She moans in pain as her body hits the ground both knees and shins now scraped and bleeding from the impact. The fear and pain make her scream again.

"Please help me! Why are you doing this?! What do you want from?!"

The sliding door slamming shut reverberates throughout the room. She drags herself toward the bowls and glances inside one of them and sees water. She ponders whether or not to drink it, but her dry pulsing throat makes the decision for her.

She gulps down the water so fast it catches in her throat causing her to cough it up, spilling some on her clothing. She grabs the second bowl and smells the contents, although it had familiar texture and color to oatmeal, the odor made her gag.

"Oh my God! That is disgusting!" In a fit of rage, she throws the bowl against the wall bouncing of the wall smashing to the ground. "I'm not an animal! Do you know who I am?! There will be people looking for me!"

No matter how angry she was or how much screaming she did, there was no response while lying on the ground, feeling helpless. She pushes her body back against the bed and sobs uncontrollably. Her eyes flash toward the door in the thought that maybe, she could force the sliding door open just a little and her screams could reach someone outside the steel door.

She rises slowly, trying to get her balance and tries to walk towards the door, but once again gets pulled to the ground due to the chain. Her anger doesn't falter as she shoots her head up.

"You motherfucker! You are going to be so sorry! You don't know who you're messing with! I know people!"

Her rants continue to go unanswered. After a few minutes the silence is interrupted by the sound of metal sliding against the outside of the door. She scurries back toward the bed. She brings her bloody knees up toward her face wrapping her arms around her bruised and scraped shins, nervously waiting as the creaking noise of the door opening amplifies in the silence.

The door finally opens, a figure stands in the doorway wearing a black hooded robe and the ominous stranger is also wearing a black, mesh mask covering its face. Every bit of skin on the stranger's body is covered including their hands. They stand in the doorway without speaking or moving for a few minutes. When the stranger finally moves the movement causes her to jump abruptly as it steps into the room closing the door and pointing down at her.

"I do know who you are and know exactly who I'm fucking with Mrs. Wilson. Or is it Miss Garfield now?"

The words frighten her as she attempts to recognize the hooded figure's voice, but it's muffled, flat, emotionless and unrecognizable to her. She stares wide-eyed at the figure, scared and attempting to put her words together, her shaking lips causes every word to stutter out.

"How...how do you know my name? What do you want?" Her voice quivers.

The hooded figure is unmoved by her words and turns away, opening the door. As the door closes behind the stranger, a response is finally given. In due time, everything will be made clear to you and all of your questions will be answered."

The sound of the metal rubbing against the outside of door tells her that the noise belongs to a slide that is keeping the door locked from the outside; once again she is left in seclusion. She screams out in frustration, "Let me go you freak!"

She lies on the floor crying before slowly picking herself off the floor and limping back up to the bed, leaving a blood trail from her wounds. When she plops down, she looks at her legs and feels excruciating pain from her ankle and knee. She rips a piece of her shirt and wipes some of the blood from her lacerations, wincing and whimpering every time the cloth touches her wounds. The pain becomes overwhelming, so she stops and lies back on the bed trying to think how could this happen to her. Trying to make sense of everything that is happening, in her weaken state she closes her eyes. Just as she begins to drift off, a scream startles her awake. It sounded like a girl screaming in agony. She sits up waiting for it to happen again. When nothing happens, she yells hoping that somebody might hear her.

"Help! Please! Can you hear me?! I'm in here!"

She listens intently, when the sound she didn't want to hear resonates through the room as the hooded figure decides to re-emerge. Immediately, she tries to reason with it, hoping that somewhere beneath that disguise there is some compassion. "Please, whoever you are just let me go. I won't tell anyone anything, please just let me go."

The hooded figure doesn't acknowledge her plea for compassion and walks over first picking up the water bowl. It then walks over to the far corner picking up the now dented bowl, the mysterious contents scattered beside it. Before leaving with the bowls in hand, the figure turns toward her speaking to her in the same muffled and emotionless voice.

"Please Miss Garfield or may I call you Deborah? I hope I can. As you heard you now have a neighbor, so you shouldn't feel so alone. You both have so much in common. I will introduce you both later."

She looks up at the hooded figure, trying to grasp why this is happening with tears in her eyes.

"Why are you doing this? What have I done to you?"

The hooded figure exits without acknowledging her words. Then just like before once the door slams shut and the lock slides close does Deborah finally hear a response to her question.

"Time will answer all, so be patient and enjoy your accommodations."

The answer does not ease Deborah's mind, she begins to tremor with fear and curls up into the fetal position. She sobs and feels more vulnerable with every passing minute. She eventually cries herself to sleep.

# CHAPTER 2

Having lost all concept of time, Deborah awakens abruptly in a cold sweat sitting up thinking that everything was just a nightmare until the pain from her ankle lets her know it's all too real. Deborah places her hands on her face trying to remember how this could have happened to her. Her memory is hazy, but slowly tries to focus on the last thing, which was her weekly shopping trip…

She remembers going to the mall and her driver dropping her off at the south entrance; her normal shopping time in the mall would be around three hours. The day was like any other shopping trip until she exited the mall carrying the usual amount of shopping bags from various boutiques. She reaches the curb and sees her white luxury SUV parked against the far wall near the loading dock. her dark tinted windows does not allow her to see whether her driver is sleeping in the vehicle.

She waited impatiently for her driver to bring her vehicle up to her. After waiting for a few minutes, she decides to walk over to the SUV's rear passenger door waiting for her driver to come out and open the door. When he doesn't come out, she yells out for him.

"Hey, asshole! Wake up and open the door!"

Deborah has never been a person who is used to be kept waiting, so she drops the bag on the ground, walks around to the driver door and pulls on door handle. She finds her car is unlocked and the driver is not in the vehicle.

"Are you fucking kidding?! Where the hell is this idiot?"

Scanning around the parking lot looking for her driver she takes a deep breath in frustration and screams, "He is so fucking fired!"

She is infuriated as her face turns red, she presses the button on the door panel to unlock the rest of the doors returning to the rear passenger door pulling it open. She looks around the parking lot a final time; her fury becomes an eruption of expletives.

"When I find you, I'm going to make your life fucking miserable. You fucking asshole!"

Patrons walk by and mumble to themselves watching her profanity-laced tirade. Satisfied with her last outburst she turns to pick up her bags when an arm reaches out from the opened door, places a rag over her mouth and yanks her into the SUV. She struggles, waving her arms wildly trying to rip the person's hand away from her mouth. Her struggles slowly diminish as she passes out and she is pulled into the back seat followed by the door slamming shut.

Deborah shakes her head but no matter how hard she tries, her recollection stops right at that point. The noise of the slide lock jars her mind back to her present predicament and the unknown stranger re-enters the room facing her.

"So are you enjoying your accommodations?" asking with a slight chuckle, while extending its arm to emphasize the surrounding,

Deborah slides to the edge of the bed and barks out, "What do you want from me?"

Dropping its arms to its side, the stranger walks toward her. "What do I want from you? I want nothing from you." It raises its arm and points at Deborah. "It's about what I'm going to give you. I'm going to give you something special, something that will change your life forever."

Deborah is about to respond, but instead watches the hooded figure turn and walk toward the far wall of the room to a section that seems slightly different than the rest of it. She hadn't notice it before probably because of the dim lighting. She watches the stranger reach out and lift a square two foot by two foot board off the wall. The board had been camouflaged within the wall, when the figure backs away it uncovers a television and a camera sitting on top of it.

Deborah stammers as she tries to speak. "Wha...what is that for?"

The hooded figure takes the dark board and responds briefly while exiting. "Very soon you will get to meet your new neighbor."

The lock slides shut and Deborah swings her legs over the bed again. She winces in pain looking down at her ankle; it has swollen and is turning a bluish purple. She lifts her leg onto the bed using minimal force to try and slip the shackle off her foot, pausing due to the pain. A small buzzing sound causes her to look up toward the television, there are no images.

Suddenly the television monitor flickers, showing grayish static along with the buzzing noise. The added light from the television brightens the room slightly. Using it to her advantage she scans the walls carefully looking for more hidden or camouflaged boards. No matter how hard she looks around all the extra lighting seems to  do is accentuate the fact that there are no windows, no other doors, just dirty, rough walls keeping her trapped in her private hell.

The buzzing noise emanating from the television seems to be getting louder and louder until the noise because unbearable making her unable to hear even her own thoughts. She falls back onto the bed covering her ears with the palms of her hands screaming.

"Please shut it off! Shut it off! Please just shut it off!"

Deborah rolls back and forth, yelling waiting for the annoying noise to stop. Even though it seemed like it would never end, the noise abruptly stops and the television screen turns completely black. She slowly removes her hands from her ears, sits up and looks toward the screen. She wipes the tears off her dirty stained face, pushing her mangled hair away from her face and unexpectedly the television turns on again.

This time, there's no sound at all, the only image on the screen is of a space similar to Deborah's room. The only difference is that there appears to be a large chair in the middle of that room. It also appears that there is a person sitting in the chair covered by a white sheet as she can see something moving under the sheet.

Staring at the screen intensely, her eyes open wide as the hooded figure makes an appearance on the screen. The hooded figure looks up toward the camera waving as it grabs a corner of the sheet and slowly pulls it off while walking off screen. Deborah gradually rises from the bed. A lump forms in her throat and her hand trembles as they cover her lips as a scream escapes.

"Oh my God—Ariel! Please, don't hurt her! Please don't hurt my daughter!"

The image on the television shows a much younger woman with wavy brown hair in her mid-twenties, wearing a light blue blouse, dark colored jeans and no shoes. She is strapped into the chair and gagged and is furiously moving from side to side, trying to get loose.

Deborah screams frantically as she lunges toward the television hoping her words can be heard. The chain causes her to crumble to the floor, doing more damaged to her already bloody appendage. In her frantic state the pain is almost nonexistent as she looks up from the ground screaming.

"Let her go you bastard!"

Deborah becomes crazed as she sits up screaming and relentlessly pulling on the shackle watching her flesh rip away from her ankle. Her adrenaline takes over, blocking the pain.

"Let her go!" She begs for answers reaching out toward the television. "Please, Why? Why are you doing this?"

Tears roll down her cheeks as she gazes at her daughter struggling in the chair. In her distraught state she fails to realize that the door has open and the hooded figure has re-entered the room. When she realizes its presence in the room her anger is direct toward her abductor.

"What do you want with my daughter? You let her go now!"

She drags her body back toward the bed, losing all faith that anyone is coming to help them. Deborah struggles to stand as the hooded figure walks over, stands next to the television and points to the image of her daughter on the screen.

"I didn't want you to be alone, since you two are so close," it says with a laugh.

Deborah is finally able to make it up to the bed, trying to compose herself, hoping that changing her tactic might help her and her daughter get released. Her first thought is this is about money so she decides to try that approach.

"Why are you doing this to us? Just tell me what you want and how much it will take to let us go. I have money."

Not getting a reaction from the stranger causes her to rethink her approach as the hooded figure walks slowly toward her. She lowers her head afraid to make eye contact with her abductor as it looms over her staring down at her.

"You see, that's your problem, you think you can solve all your problems with money. Today money won't help you or your daughter. You see, I want you to feel pain. I want you to feel anguish. I want you to feel helpless."

"What have I ever done to you?" Deborah pleads slowly raising her head and reaching out her hand to touch her captor.

Deborah hopes that compassion and her physical contact will help her get out of this situation. Before her hand touches it, the stranger raises its arm and backs away from her.

"I said everything will be explained to you. You will very soon receive a history lesson that will bring everything to light."

With those words, the hooded figure exits. Deborah looks and feels completely defeated sitting on the bed, while looking at the television screen that has gone blank. It sends her into another rage.

"Ariel, if you can hear me, be strong! Everything will be okay, honey! Ariel, can you hear me?!"

When she hears no response Deborah begins to rock nervously back and forth on the bed. Then suddenly, the room illuminates once again as the television turns on, but the image on the screen is not of her daughter. Instead, it's video recording footage from outside of the Johnston mall.

This is the mall that Deborah and Ariel spent countless hours, sometimes twice a week on their mother and daughter outings, shopping and getting their hair and nails done. Deborah watches as the video now cuts away showing them getting their makeovers inside Cheek's salon and has no problem recalling this day.

Now she wonders if the person who recorded them, the same person underneath the mask or if it was more than one person. How long were we being followed? She slaps her hands over her face, her mind is deluged with so many thoughts that cause her to lash out and begin punching the bed repeatedly in frustration.

"Who the hell are you? Why were you following us? What do you want from us?"

The video stops abruptly and returns back to Ariel sitting in the room. The figure reappears in the room, slowly walking behind Ariel leaning over grabbing Ariel pale tear stricken face with its gloved hands turning her head forcibly to look up at the camera. Ariel struggles in the chair fighting against the restraints, but slowly ceases as she weakens.

"You leave my daughter alone, you monster! Get the fuck away from her!" Deborah knows by now that she can't be heard, but her maternal instincts tell her to keep yelling to protect her daughter.

The hooded figure releases Ariel's face and gently brushes her hair off her red cheeks and strokes them. The hooded figure places its head next to Ariel's face and looks up at the camera. "Beauty is so important to you and your daughter."

Ariel tries her best to shake her head but the figure grabs her face roughly to steady it while continuing to look up at the camera. Deborah is irate seeing everything her daughter is enduring with this unknown entity.

"You fucking bastard, leave her alone!"

Before it releases its grip the figure whispers into Ariel ear. "I believe your ugliness goes deep within you so let's see if we can't do something to get the outside to match your inside."

Releasing her face, the figure stands up straight and speaks directly into the camera.

"Let's find out how deep Ariel's ugliness really goes."

Deborah stares at the television not understanding its words, but fears the worst seeing the figure slowly step over to a silver file cabinet with several rust patches. The figure slides open the top drawer. Ariel tries to turn her head to look toward the sound of the grinding metal of the opening file cabinet, as the figure meticulously pulls a pair of long, silver scissors.

Once the scissors are completely taken out of the drawer, the figure turns walking back into camera view, opening and closing the scissors. The noise causes Ariel to shake furiously in the chair fearing the oncoming sound of the scissors. Deborah on the other hand wobbles as she stands off the bed seeing exactly what this creature is holding in its hand.

The hooded figure saunters toward Ariel, setting its sights on her wavy brown locks. The figure stands behind the chair brushing her hair way from her face, abruptly grabbing a large section of hair pulling it taut and placing the hair within the scissors blades. Ariel's eyes turn toward the glimmer of the sheers, which instinctively causes her to struggle against her straps.

Knowing what's about to come next, Deborah screams and pleads towards the monitor. "No! Stop, please! Please!"

But no matter how much Deborah pleas or cries, the hooded figure begins to slowly cut away at her daughter's hair, dropping the loose chunks on the floor.

"You are nothing but a monster, you fucking bastard!" Deborah screams.

Throughout Deborah's imprisonment she has screamed out for help, yelled profanities at her captor never getting much of a response. On this occasion her words have caused the figure to stop cutting her daughter's hair and stare back at the camera, acknowledging her words.

"You dare call me a bastard, a monster. Have you ever looked in a mirror? Has your daughter?"

The figure laughs, shaking its head as it turns its attention back to Ariel's brown wavy hair. Tears roll down Ariel's cheeks and the front of her gag as she watches in horror as some of her hair floats to the ground like weightless feathers. The figure is now grabbing some of the cut pieces off her shoulders and throwing them up in the air, while speaking with anger toward the camera.

"You and your daughter are the worst type of monsters. You bring misery to people's lives and then you feed off it."

The figure drops the scissors to the grounds and points directly toward the camera. Ariel, choking on her tears, is completely drained of energy both physically and emotionally, leaving her unable to struggle.

"You are narcissistic, greedy, cruel bitches! It's about time you both experience the pain you've caused others!"

As the hooded figure turns the screen goes black. Deborah is left in the dark, not knowing what will happen to her daughter next. She continues to plead to the television, wishing for all this to just stop.

"Why are you doing this? Please just leave her alone."

She stands awaiting some sort of response from this unidentified evil, but the screen stays blank, her calm tone begins to gravitate back into frenzy.

"We haven't done anything to anyone! Do you hear me?!

Her words just echo in the silence as she slumps down onto the bed, her anger fading slowly into the dark abyss.

# CHAPTER 3

The hooded stranger walks down a murky hallway that is dimly lit similar to the other rooms that are holding Deborah and Ariel. The stranger's footsteps are the only sound that can be heard until it reaches its destination. Another rusted steel door with a slide lock on the other side of the door sits a barber-style chair that is bolted into the ground. In the chair sits a man in his mid-forties with short salt and pepper colored hair and wearing nothing but a white T-shirt and blue boxer shorts.

The man is being held by leather restraints that are strapped around his wrist, ankles, chest and thighs. The only part of his body that is not restrained is his head, which gives his neck full mobility. The mobility means nothing when he come to and realizes he can't see anything. His head is throbbing when he awakens and it becomes obvious to him that he is blindfolded and unable to see his surroundings.

When he attempts to get up he begins to realize that something is preventing him from doing so. He becomes more concerned in his situation realizing that his entire body has been restrained into the chair. He begins to squirm in the chair fighting against the restraints. "Hello?! Can anyone hear me?!"

He suddenly stops his thrashing around when he hears the sound of metal scraping against metal. The hooded stranger has finally decided to make an appearance in the room opening the door slowly and entering. With stealth, the stranger creeps behind his chair. Unsure if someone is around him, the man in the chair turns his head in the direction of the unlocking door.

He listens intently for any other sounds that might indicate someone might have heard his scream. After waiting a few seconds and without hearing a sound, he begins moving his head from side to side as he feels that he is no longer alone.

"Who's there? Answer me damn it, I'm a cop!"

He feels the eerie aura of a person standing somewhere nearby and continues to twist his head in a vain attempt to ascertain who is behind him. He attempts to rub his head against the edge of the chair hoping it would pull up his blindfold. The hooded figure stands still, merely observing the man's struggles. The figure then decides to make its presence known. It reaches out, grabbing hold of the man face and leans forward to his ear. "Hello Mr. Gibson," it whispers. "It's nice to see you again even though you can't say the same."

Gibson attempts to shake his head to break the stranger's grip.

"Who are you and what the hell do you want?!"

The hooded figure releases his face and walks around the chair as Gibson turns his head, following the sound of the stranger's monotone unrecognizable voice.

"In due time Mr. Gibson. Oh, I'm sorry it's Detective Gibson isn't it? But then again calling you detective is such disrespect to *real* detectives."

The figure stops in front of him, watching him struggle with the restraints; amused as Det. Gibson shakes side to side yelling in anger.

"Fuck you, you asshole! They will be looking for me! You can't get away with this!"

The angry taunts do nothing to affect the hooded figure's demeanor who strolls toward the wall in front of the chair. There sits a cart underneath a dingy, raggedy white sheet. Reaching under the sheet and grabbing a handle, the stranger pulls the cart. The noise of the screeching wheels bring a sense of panic from Det. Gibson as he once again tries to rub his head against the head rest cushion trying to get the blindfold off his face.

Setting the cart beside Det. Gibson chair this malevolent being briefly stops and stares down at him, even though he can't see Det. Gibson feels someone's presence is again near him.

"Talk to me damn it! What do you want?!"

The figure continues looking at him, moving its head from side to side pondering what to do. "All your questions will soon be answered, but you must understand as the host of this little private party, I must welcome all my guests in a timely fashion."

With a slight laugh, the figure walks out of the room slamming the door. The noise from the door and the sliding lock echoes throughout the room, jolting Det. Gibson.

"Hey! What guests?! What the fuck are you talking about?! Are you still there? Talk to me!"

The lack of any response causes him for the first time since awakening to feel afraid. The light begins to flicker on and off which has no effect on him due to his blindfold and he sits, drenched in his own cold sweat completely abandoned. For now...

# CHAPTER 4

An ambulance-type stretcher can be seen in the center of the dimly lit room similar to the other rooms where the stranger's other guests are being held. There is a strong musty smell emanating from the windowless room, the walls consist of the similar gray bricks as the others. Lying on the stretcher is a frail looking man strapped down by his ankles, wrists, chest and thighs.

He is wearing a short-sleeve shirt that at one point was white, but due to the perspiration and dirt stains it is now a blackish grey. His pants are torn at the knee, stained with dirt and were rolled up to his shins exposing both of his feet, which are deprived of socks and shoes.

As the man begins to stir on the stretcher, he tries to sit up only to find that something is holding him down. He looks down and sees that parts of his body are tied to this stretcher by some sort of straps. He tries again to sit up this time straining a little harder struggling against the restraints, but he doesn't have the strength to get loose.

"Where am I?" He asks out loud as he looks around the room moving his head; the only body part that was not immobilized. He tries once again to fight against the restraints by shaking his limbs trying to loosen them, but again the restraints are so tight they begin to leave an indentation in his skin. Fear begins to take over and like the others he doesn't waste any time screaming for help.

"Hello! Can anybody hear me?! I need help!"

Also like the others, all the shouting is just a waste of breath as his screams are swallowed by the brick walls. Then the familiar sound of a steel lock sliding against a metal door ceases his fidgeting and he turns his head in the direction of the noise but he sees nothing. Then he hears footsteps making their way towards him. Sheer excitement spreads through him as he believes that his screams have been heard and help has arrived.

"Thank god! You heard me! Can you please release these straps?"

Anxiously waiting to be freed he doesn't understand why he hasn't been released from his makeshift prison. All the while as he waits to be released, his savior happens to be the hooded figure, who is standing behind the stretcher, silently admiring the man's expectation of freedom.

"What are you waiting for? Please untie me!"

He tries to look behind him, but unfortunately the strap across his chest makes the effort worthless. Suddenly a pair of black gloved hands reaches down onto the man's shoulders, causing him to squeal out in fear. As he looks up toward the ceiling, he sees a black hood and a black mesh mask looking down at him.

"Jesus Christ, who are you?!"

Chuckling at the man's reaction, the hooded figure releases its pressurizing grip on the man's bony shoulders and begins to stroll around the stretcher, stopping at the foot of the stretcher looking down at him. Not uttering a word, when suddenly the silence is broken.

"Hey, what's up, Doc? I've always wanted to say that," the hooded figure says with a chuckle. Just as quickly as the laughter starts it stops and the figure continues staring at the cowardly man. The man's heart is thumping in terror and he tries to slow his breathing so he can try to form a sentence.

"W-w...What do you want from me?"

The question causes the hooded figure to shake its head in frustration.

"All of you are so impatient, after all the trouble that I have gone through to make these arrangements. But that's okay since you are my last guest; we can now begin Dr. Levitt."

Raising his head, afraid to look up at this faceless stranger, but he finally gets the courage to look at this person. He is unsure if it's the figure's menacing stance or the dark colored robe that amplifies its real stature. But it really didn't matter how big or small the person was at this point, he was helpless to do anything and there were still many questions that needed to be answered.

"What do you mean begin? What do you want with me?"

Ignoring him yet again the figure jaunts toward the farthest wall in the room. Just like before, the hooded figure begins to remove a large board that had been camouflaged in the wall. Once the board is removed a camera mounted on top of a television is now visible. Already confused and afraid because of his current state, the appearance of the camera and television does nothing to ease Dr. Levitt's mind.

"Please tell me what you want? I just don't understand why I'm here?" Dr. Levitt pleads, trying to speak in between his tears that are now leaving streaks on his face.

But his tears and pleas do nothing to affect his captor who points towards the television while looking at Dr. Levitt who is now a blubbering mess. The figure lowers its arm and walks slowly toward the stretcher; Dr. Levitt looks away in fear. Reaching down and grabbing Dr. Levitt face forcing him to look at its captor, who places its right index finger close to where a mouth would be on the mesh mask signaling Dr. Levitt to quiet down.

Not knowing what might happen to him if he doesn't follow instruction; he begins to take slower breaths and tries to regain some kind of composure despite his hyperventilating state. Looking like a puffer fish as he tries to slow his breathing his cheeks puff out as his crying now sounds more like a puppy dog whimpering.

"Thank you Dr. Levitt. Now that I have your attention, what I was trying to tell you is that you will be seeing the rest of my guests very soon. But to answer your earlier question, what do I want from you? The answer is nothing. It's what I'm going to give you all."

Dr. Levitt turns away from his captor and looks over at the television confused and still not understanding why he is being held prisoner. With those parting words the hooded figure walks toward the door as Dr. Levitt begins his crying and pleading once again.

"Please just let me go! I don't understand what you want!"

Without uttering a word the door slams close.

# CHAPTER 5

Tears run continuously down Ariel's puffy, red cheeks. She has been sobbing uncontrollably, struggling against her restraints and feeling hopeless. The burning and throbbing pain she feels causes her to stop her movement, slumping her head forward causes loose brown clumps of her hair to fall onto her lap. She squeezes her eyes tight trying to recall any memory of how she arrived in this hell. The last thing she remembers is being outside the Palm's Night Club; one of her regular hot spots where she was well known and so loved the attention she would often receive.

That evening she spent the entire evening dancing and having drinks with a few of her closest friends, a typical girl's night out. Around 1:00 a.m. she told them she was leaving giving each other air kisses on each cheek and went outside into the breezy, cool air. As soon as she walks up to the valet station the two valets stumble over each trying to outrush each other to get her car. She enjoyed seeing them fuss over her and smiled as they ran to get her car. She soon grew impatient after a waiting few minutes and began pacing back and forth.

Her ire grows with every passing minute; it increases as men she considered to not be in her league begin their pathetic advances toward her. Irritated by the wait and the propositions, she turned to re-enter the club to complain. Suddenly a sharp pinch hit on her backside cause her to spin around to see who would have the audacity to touch her, when her vision starts to become blurry. She grabs her head, wobbling in her heels and begins to lose her balance.

*Why is everything spinning?*

At that exact moment a car pulls up in front of her and she is unable to make out if it's her car. She also can't make out the identity of the person next to her who is speaking. She heard them talking, but can't recall a face.

"I'll take the keys. My friend had a little too much to drink."

The valet hands the keys to this stranger and held the car door open as the stranger placed Ariel into the passenger side of the car.

Ariel still incoherent and unable to focus looked over toward the driver's side and she saw a blurry hand reaching over pulling down her seatbelt clicking it in place. She tried to raise her hand to fight off the blurry image but was not able to. She opened her mouth in an attempt to scream, but all her words are slurred and unintelligible. As the car pulled off, her head rolled back and forth against the headrest. She glanced over and still could not distinguish who the intruder was.

The last detail she could remember are the words the unknown captor leaned in and whispered to her that night.

"Hi, remember me? Don't worry. It will all come back to you very soon!"

The emotions of remembering that awful night resurfaced, she becomes angry and thrashes around in the chair. All of her movements break the dead silence as her anger has caused a boost of adrenaline giving her the brief strength to shake violently from side to side trying to get free and to scream through the gag hoping for salvation.

But the rush of adrenaline does not last long as her outburst slowly begins to dissipate and the only sound that Ariel hears is that of her sniveling accompanied by her panting breath, which eventually turns to complete silence.

# CHAPTER 6

Detective Gibson has tried everything to set himself free. Each new idea to free himself from the unbearable straps causes him to feel more angry and frustrated with each failed attempt. Unable to free himself he sits there and begins to recall the events leading up to his current journey through the depths of hell.

He begins to remember his daily trip to Carlos's Bodega, the place where he went daily to eat three times a day. He went twice for his daily fix of coffee, and for his usual lunch consisting of a turkey and cheese hero and an orange soda. Even though the bodega was two blocks from the station house, he would always take his car since he enjoyed listening to the sport station while he ate his lunch. Det. Gibson shakes his head as he recalls bits and piece of his last day of freedom.

Like any day during lunch time, he strolled out of Carlos's Bodega and strolled to his car with his lunch in his hand. This started a chain of events that would change his life. As soon as he grabbed the driver's side door handle he felt a deep burning sensation in the palm of his right hand. It began to burn like a small eruption of fire in his palm.

He dropped his lunch on the ground and rubbed his hand on his navy blue pants. The more his skin felt like it was on fire. After a few minutes the burning feeling subsided but his right arm began to feel numb. The numbness started to course throughout his body. It caused his body to stiffen and not able to move his arm to reach his phone.

He began to feel groggy and his body fell forward against his car. That was when he heard someone approach him from behind. He could not move his head or body to see who was behind him leaving him feeling completely vulnerable.

Det. Gibson could sense a presence behind him and when he tried to open his mouth he realized that even that movement has been restricted. His body was completely useless, except for his eyes that darted back and forth trying to ascertain who was nearby. That was when he saw a figure from the left corner of his eye and the back door of his car being opened. This person grabbed him from behind and shoved him into the backseat of the car.

Before the door slammed shut, he heard a faint voice.

"Hi Tim, don't get up. Get some rest. I want you well rested for the party." The person laughed as Det. Gibson lay on the backseat staring at the floor of his car before everything went black.

The flashback causes his face to turn red as his veins bulge against his neck in anger and he strains against the restraints lashing out.

"Whoever you are, you are fucking with the wrong guy! You hear me?!"

# CHAPTER 7

From the moment the hooded figure exited the room and the door closed, Dr. Levitt has not stopped sniveling and pleading for someone to come help him. With every passing moment he felt his energy and hope for rescue slowly began to fade away, he mumbles to himself, asking how he ended up in this room.

The last image he recalls is leaving his office, getting into his car and driving to his favorite after work stop, the Aura Lounge, for Happy Hour. The Aura Lounge is a dimly lit place with a clientele of both younger and middle class professionals. But Happy Hour on Thursday and Friday night, the Lounge offers drink specials that bring in a younger crowd, which was the main reason Dr. Levitt was there.

He remembers walking to his regular table in the back of the lounge away from most of the patrons and doing what he enjoys the most during Happy Hour: watching the young girls walking around in their short and revealing clothing. He settled into his seat as an attractive waitress walked over to his table and placed his favorite drink on the table.

"Here you go, sir—Harvey Wallbanger," she said in a cheerful tone.

He looked up at her, bewildered. "I'm sorry madam but I have yet to order anything."

The waitress smiled and turned pointing toward the bar which was then overflowing with patrons. Her finger extended out toward the bar, but due to the crowd and the poor lighting he did not recognize anyone there.

"The bartender told me to deliver this drink to you. He said your secret admirer claimed you had treated them in the past and just wanted to thank you."

Dr. Levitt continued to survey the area around the lounge for any familiar face. Just as the waitress was about to take the drink back, he grabbed the drink, smiled, and raised the glass.

"Well we can't let this go to waste. Cheers to my secret admirer."

He guzzled down the drink and ordered another as soon as the glass hit the table. Dr. Levitt continued drinking for another forty-five minutes, all the while gawking at all the voluptuous young women milling around the lounge.

As he raised his hand to get the attention of waitress for his fifth drink, he began feeling dizzy and light headed. The room started spinning and all the attractive women had become blurry figures moving within the dim light of the lounge.

"Why is the room spinning? I've only had four drinks," he said to himself as he squeezed his forehead.

At that moment a blurry image approached his table.

"You don't look so good, friend. I think you need some help."

Dr. Levitt's tried to answer the person, but by now his words are short and mumbled his ability to form a complete sentence was gone. The stranger reached down and helped him up out of his seat wrapping an arm around Dr. Levitt's waist. At that moment the waitress returned showing concern about Dr. Levitt condition.

"Is he okay?"

"Yeah my friend just drank a little too much. Don't worry; I'll get him home safe."

The stranger paid Dr. Levitt's bill and tipped the waitress a fifty dollar bill, which brought a grin to her face. She suggested a hangover remedy, wished them a safe trip home and a good night before going back to the bar. At a slow pace, the stranger walked toward the front door with Dr. Levitt in tow; almost dragging his body to a nearby car and put him into the backseat.

Once the stranger was in the driver's seat, they turned to look down at Dr. Levitt's semi-conscious limp body spread across the back seat.

"Hey doc, aren't you lucky you have a designated driver? Because you know you should never drink and drive."

The stranger let out a laugh before pulling into traffic and speeding off into the night.

Reliving that night brings fear and helplessness as the doctor screams at the top of his lungs.

"For the love of God, someone please help me!"

But like all the other guests, the screams eventually are followed by echoes that fade into the silence of the darkness. Suddenly the silence is broken as a voice booms over a loud speaker, blasting into all the rooms.

"I would like to welcome all my guests to our little reunion. On this day many years ago, lives were changed forever, so I felt it only proper that we all got together to celebrate. You have all claimed to have done nothing; that this is all a mistake. But you all have cheated, humiliated, lied and destroyed people's lives—something that is normal behavior for all you. But today each of you is going to re-live history. Each of you will understand pain, cruelty and eventually death."

The sounds of all of them screaming can be heard coming from all the rooms as the hooded figure walks along the darken hallway enjoying the panic in their voices.

# CHAPTER 8

Ariel had been crying nonstop through her ordeal, but hearing those ominous words has her hyper-ventilating through her gag. She knows her breathing has to calm to prevent herself from choking. She hears the sound of the sliding lock opening. She turns her head and catches a glimpse of her jailer walking into the room not looking or acknowledging her hysterical state.

Ariel thrashes against her restraints attempting to yell through her gag to gain its attention. She abruptly stops all her movements seeing that her jailer is walking toward the wall and removing something from it. A board that had been cleverly hidden within the wall is completely removed, that's when a television is exposed and it's underneath the camera that had been trained on her. The stranger turns on the television and walks toward Ariel.

Her attention shifts from the television to the black shadow now standing in front of her. She turns her face away and attempts to move her body despite being restrained, trying to distance herself from this unholy person that is holding her prisoner. All of her movement ceases when she catches a glimpse of the image on the television screen. It's her mother, sitting on the floor, crying and bleeding from her legs. Ariel can't believe what she is seeing; the figure bends down toward eye level and caresses her right cheek gently.

"You see you're not alone. I did say it was a get together."

Ariel's shakes her head trying to remove its hand from her face, turning red as she screams into her gag. Her captor stands back admiring her wild and fighting spirit, then raises a finger placing it on the gag, pushing the gag deeper into her mouth causing her to begin choking as she struggles to get air. Her captor begins stroking her face, not even reacting to her difficulty in breathing.

"There, there…Your mother can't hear you. Even if you weren't gagged, your screams would go unheard. Now you know how it feels to scream and wait for somebody to come to your rescue, until you realize nobody cares and nobody is coming."

With those words her captor steps back and turns away from her, removing its finger from her gag listening to her cough trying to catch her breath. She slowly regains her normal breathing pattern. Fearing more reprisal from her captor, she ceases any further movements against her restraints.

When her captor turns back around, Ariel's eyes widen, her breathing accelerates and she shakes her head from side to side. The hooded figure is holding in its hand a long, shiny straight razor.

"Don't worry I just want to make sure you look your best for the reunion."

Walking and circling behind Ariel's chair, the hooded figure glances at its tool before focusing its attention back to Ariel. She turns her head away fighting in her chair as the razor comes closer to her, but all her struggles are for nothing. Her head is grabbed roughly as laughter erupts with the very first stroke against her head.

"Don't move your head. You wouldn't want to lose an ear."

The first stroke on her dry scalp is deep as it scrapes along her scalp causing a streak of blood to flow down the side of her pulsating head. She struggles against its powerful grip causing the razor to cut deeper into her scalp, more blood oozing from her scalp and sliding down every clear path on her face.

She begins convulsing in pain, her toes and feet curl with every bloody stroke that is made on her head. Her face is slowly turning into a crimson mess as the blood seeps down her face saturating her clothes.

The hooded figure ceases briefly and glances down at its blood-stained blade.

"You see? I was doing such a good job and you made me slip," the captor said in a matter of fact tone. It removes a piece of flesh from the edge of the razor and wipes some of the excess blood using its robe.

"Now don't move. I'm almost done."

Her muffled cries and coughs continue as the taste of blood drips into her mouth through the gag.

"Oh my, can't have you choke on your own blood."

In a weird moment of compassion, the captor pulls out a rag, wiping some of the blood from around her eyes, nose and around the gag. Then tossing the rag on the ground it takes a few steps back admiring its work like an artist in awe after completing a masterpiece.

"Ta–dah, I'm all done!!"

Some of Ariel's tears wash away some of the blood remnants from her stained cheeks, leaving pale and maroon lines on her face. She tries to mouths words through her gag again and is finally able to push out one word.

"Why?"

Ignoring her question her captor picks up the rag and wipes more of Ariel's blood off the razor.

"I'm so sorry I was busy cleaning up. Are you asking me why?" The hooded figure asks, sarcastically.

Lethargic from the pain, she manages to nod. Her eyes follow the figure's movements as it extends its arm pointing toward the image on the television. She slowly tilts her head up trying to see through her blurred vision the image of her mother still sobbing on the ground.

"You see today is an important day. A day your mother created along with you and the others!!"

Ariel head slumps in pain and desperation knowing that not even her mother can help her. She begins whimpering as the hooded figure walks toward the door, stopping briefly in front of Ariel.

"So how do you like your hair cut? Well, I'll be back later to finish the rest of your makeover. Don't you run off now, you hear."

The hooded figure turns off the TV and exits the room.

# CHAPTER 9

Deborah's throat is hoarse from all the screaming. Somehow, she still finds the drive and the strength to endure all the pain involved in trying to remove the shackle from her very swollen bloody ankle. When a piece of flesh becomes entangled within the shackle, she screams and releases the shackle right away.

She pulls her free leg up onto the bed and lays her restless head against her knee. All of a suddenly she hears a sound that cause her to raise her head. The noise is coming from outside the door. Thinking that her jailer is about to reenter the room her body begins to shiver in fear, when the small metal door at the bottom slides opens. Once again, two silver bowls are pushed into the room; she looks down at them as the door slides close.

She hesitates slightly before sliding down off the bed to get down on the ground and crawl toward the bowls. She reaches out for one bowl and the contents bring a needed relief to her as it contains water. She gulps it down coughing up some of it, spilling a majority of it on her shirt in an attempt to quench her dry, sore throat.

Once she makes sure that she has drank every drop of water out of the bowl, she places it on the concrete then reaches out for the second bowl. The contents of this bowl bring about curiosity it looks similar to the content from earlier, but the smell is tolerable. She sticks her finger into the tan colored substance, this time hoping that this substance is actually edible.

She scoops up a small amount on the tip of her finger and places it on the tip of her tongue trying to get her taste buds to identify this mush like substance. She's surprised her taste buds flare up in an excited frenzy, her tongue actually responds positively to the substance is as it appears to be oatmeal.

Deborah has no clue how long she's been held prisoner, but she does know her body's desperately craves food. She uses her hands as utensils quickly scooping up handful of the oatmeal from the bowl. After her first few handfuls she stops and stares at her hands shaking her head not believing to the depths she has lowered herself. But the hunger wipes away the thoughts of pride and ego and she continues to scoop handfuls of her nourishment. Once the bowl is empty she begins licking the remaining morsels from her fingertips.

Just as she is about to lick the inside of the bowl the familiar sound of the slide lock opening and the steel door opening causes her to stop as her jailer re-emerges back in the room. She pushes herself back against the bed still holding onto the bowl. Her lips tremble as she looks up at her jailer, who appears larger than life from her current position.

"Don't worry Fido; I'm not going to take your food."

The hooded figure looks at her pathetically and laughs. Those comments enrage her causing her to hurl the bowls toward her captor.

"You motherfucker, I'm not a dog."

The lack of strength makes dodging the bowl effortless as the sound of the metal bowl slamming against the wall echoes in the room. Even though the bowl did not make contact it took the attempt as an insult making the hooded figure step forward and place its right foot on top of her injured ankle—causing her to scream in agony. Looking down at her, the hooded figure makes sure all its weight is being placed on her injured ankle.

"That was not nice. Deborah. You have such a bad temper. You're right. You're not a dog. You hate dogs don't you, Deborah?"

After what seems like an eternity of having its weight pressing down on her ankle, the hooded figure removes its foot and Deborah immediately retracts her leg inward.

She immediately grabs the shackle and sees that it has penetrated her skin and has caused another deep gash on her ankle. She's screams out in pain and pulls the shackle out of the wound. She presses down on the incision to stop the bleeding, causing even more excruciating pain. Her jailer strolls over to pick up the dented bowl, then walks near her shivering body and grabs the other bowl while looking down at her wounded leg. It removes a small black box that appears to be a remote from its robe and clicks a button on it without Deborah noticing.

"Hey I think you may need a doctor? Maybe he makes house calls," her jailer says, breaking out in laughter.

In excruciating pain and angry at this demonic person who laughs at her suffering, Deborah looks up about to begin a profanity-laced tired toward her abductor when she hears a familiar voice coming from the television. She glances toward the screen, her mouth and eyes widen when she recognizes the face of the man on the screen.

"Oh my God! Dr. Levitt!

Deborah buries her face in her hands, mortified at the sound of Dr. Levitt's screaming as he struggles against the restraints.

"Help me! Please! Someone…please!" Dr. Levitt shouts.

Deborah drags herself closer to the television trying to get a better look at him. But the chain pulls her leg back holding her in place as she extends her hand toward the television. Even though it in heart she knows he can't see or hear her, she still tries hoping that she is wrong.

"Yes, Doctor! I can hear you!"

She feels utterly hopeless at this point. She couldn't help her poor daughter during her torture now she is being force to watch someone else she knows strapped down. She doesn't know what painful acts he will have to endure.

"Aaaahhhhh! Damn you!"

Deborah's arm drops to the ground as she balls up into the fetal position sobbing uncontrollably, her body shivering both from pain and fear. As she lies there sobbing and shivering on the dirty cold floor, she doesn't realize that the television screen slowly has faded out into a snowy screen before eventually dimming to black.

# CHAPTER 10

Trapped in his own psychological prison unable to move or see his surroundings, every sound becomes more daunting, when suddenly Detective Gibson receives another jolt to his hearing as the familiar sound of the door preparing to open amplifies throughout the room. He twists his head again in the direction of the noise, but isn't able to see who entered. But his gut feeling tells him that the person who entered is his ominous jailer.

"Is that you, you fucker?!"

The hooded figure finds his comment amusing, but does not respond. Instead, silently and calmly walks to the far wall of the room removing a board off the wall uncovering a television and camera identically to the ones in all the other rooms.

Det. Gibson moves his head slowly scanning the room trying to listen for any sound as he feels that there is someone in the room with him, His captor walks around him standing in front of him staring not making a sound, then creeping toward the back of the chair. The lack of any sound is unnerving to Det. Gibson and he begins to scream out and shake violently in his chair.

"Answer me you fucking coward! I know you're still here! You are so lucky I'm tied down or I would fuck you up!"

Watching him from behind the chair amused at his outburst, the hooded figure leans forward to whisper into Det. Gibson ear. "Tsk, tsk, tsk, such hostility. What would your friends say if they heard your language?" asking with a giggle.

The hooded figure comes out from behind the chair. Det. Gibson turns his head in the direction of its voice yelling, not knowing the evil is now standing in front of him.

"Fuck you, you coward! Untie me and I will show you hostility!"

Completely ignoring his comments, the hooded figure pulls out the small remote and clicks a button turning on the television. All of Det. Gibson's struggles cease as he hears a woman voice that sounds vaguely familiar to him.

"I can't believe this is happening. Why...Why is this happening?" The voice resonates throughout the room.

Det. Gibson begins moving his head around frantically trying to gauge where the voice is coming from yelling out to the now recognizable voice.

"Deborah! Where are you?! It's me, Tim! Deborah, can you hear me?!"

Pausing slightly trying to wait for a response, all he hears is Deborah sobbing. He directs his focus now toward his abductor, who he knows is still present in the room.

"What have you done with Deborah?!"

Still standing in front of Det. Gibson, but not in a talkative mood, the hooded figure leans over to the covered cart that was placed earlier beside Det. Gibson's chair. It removes the sheet exposing a silver metal tray with a full array of shiny steel surgical knives lined out next to each other in size order. Their extreme polished effects give off an amazing sparkle even in this dim lighting.

"Tim, I'm completely insulted. I haven't done anything to anyone yet, oops I'm sorry that is not true. But anyway Tim, you have always ignored things people tell you and you only hear what you want to hear."

At that moment without hesitation this unforgiving stranger picks up several different scalpels before deciding on a large scalpel examining it carefully in the dim light.

Det. Gibson heard the sound of metal moving around beside him and begins shaking from side to side, fearing what he can't see and hoping to turn over the chair. The chair is bolted so his struggles against the chair are futile.

"What are you talking about you fucking nut?!"

Ignoring Det. Gibson's insulting tirades the hooded stranger places the scalpel back on the tray and grabs a folded leather strap that was also on the tray. Upon opening the strap it snaps it together causing a loud noise that echoes around the room making Det. Gibson's movement to cease. Every snapping motion of the leather straps causes Det. Gibson to jump in his seat in fear.

"What's that?" Det. Gibson asks nervously.

But Det. Gibson receives no answer, as the hooded figure walks around to the back of the chair and pulls the head rest from the back of the chair straight up bringing it even with Det. Gibson's head. This causes him to move his head trying to look behind him.

"What are you doing?!"

But before he can ask any more questions, the hooded figure once again snaps the leather strap and in one quick movement snaps it over Det. Gibson forehead pulling his head roughly backward toward the head rest and strapping his head securely to the head rest. Det. Gibson tries to shake his head, but the freedom he had before has now been taken away from him.

"Get off me you bastard!"

But all his yelling is completely useless as he is now completely incapacitated.

The hooded figure circles back to the tray once again picking up the large silver scalpel off the tray, placing it to the right side of Det. Gibson's head.

"Since you decide you didn't want to hear the truth before, then in reality you have no need for these," the hooded figure whispers in his ear.

Just as Det. Gibson opens his mouth to speak, in one short quick stroke, his captor slices off his right ear and tosses onto the tray.

Gibson lets out a blood curling scream trying to move his head as blood begins to flow from the right side of his head.

"Ahhhhhhh! You can't do this to me! I'm a cop!"

The blood continues to drip down the side of his head making its way down the front of his body. The sadistic being begins to laugh at the sight of his helpless, bloody state.

"You're not a cop. You stopped being a cop many years ago. Ten years ago, someone came to you pleaded with you for help, but all those cries for help went unanswered. So since you don't like to listen to the truth, you don't need either one of these."

Before Det. Gibson can say a word, the hooded figure starts on the second step of its masterpiece; Det. Gibson's left ear. This time the process is methodical grabbing the left ear and slowly slicing it moving the scalpel back and forth as if it was cutting a piece of wood. After a few agonizing moments and some horrific screams from Det. Gibson his left ear is thrown onto the tray next to his right ear. Det. Gibson is now whimpering and mumbling incoherent words, he has become a beaten bloody shell of a man.

Now that both ears have been removed this malevolent person grabs a rag and begins to clean the blood and flesh from the scalpel before setting it down on the tray. It then reaches for a bottle containing a clear liquid. This blood thirsty person stares at Det. Gibson's blood streaked face, before leaning into it.

"Can you hear me now?" the captor says, bursting into an enormous hearty laugh. "Now that's funny! I should have been a comedian. But don't you fret. I'm very conscious about what can happen to wounds if you don't take care of them and I won't let your wounds get infected."

Without hesitation the hooded figure pulls up on the nozzle from the bottle and begins to squeeze the transparent liquid all over Gibson's head, making sure the majority of the liquid hits both side of the wounds on his head. The moment the liquid come into contact with his wounds Det. Gibson begins to thrash, convulse and scream in complete agony.

Det. Gibson's convulsions cause the liquid to move around his face and deeper into the wounds causing him more insufferable pain.

"Ahhhhh!!!! Stop! Please!"

Once all the contents of the bottle have been used and the bottle is completely empty the bottle is tossed onto the tray.

"That's the thing with alcohol. It helps prevent infection but it stings like a bitch doesn't it? What type of host would I be if I let you die before your time? Why that would be so rude."

With those parting words the hooded figure walks toward the door stopping briefly before exiting looking over at Det. Gibson's bloody pathetic whimpering body.

"Now remember don't go dying on me. Toodles."

# CHAPTER 11

It has been quite a while since Dr. Levitt had seen or heard from his abductor, causing him to think has he been left here to die. He was despaired at the deafening silence in this makeshift prison with no means of escape. He stared up at the bugs circling around the lone light bulb with the recurring image of the faceless hooded stranger holding him prisoner.

Dr. Levitt becomes lost in his thought fearing what else this ghastly person will do to him, when he is brought back to reality at the sound of the slide lock opening. It brings him to a new level of trepidation. Dr. Levitt hears the footsteps entering the room, but there is something else besides the footsteps that he hears— an irritating screeching sound of something scraping against the floor.

He cocks his head up to bravely peek over toward the sound and what he sees brings a chill through his body. The hooded figure is dragging something that is covered with a white sheet. Whatever the item is, it is being pulled closer to toward him. The mysterious item is placed by the foot of the stretcher and the ominous stranger exits the room without uttering a word.

Seconds seems like minutes, which then feel like hours before the faceless captor re-enters the room carrying a steel stool with a black seat. The captor places the stool by the head of the stretcher taking a seat and staring down at a quivering Dr. Levitt.

"So how are we doing doctor?" It asks cheerful manner.

Tears form in Dr. Levitt eyes as he begins to plead with his faceless captor again.

"Please just let me go. I won't tell anyone I promise."

Unmoved by Dr. Levitt's words it reaches out to the white sheet and pulls it off exposing a large black box with four black cables exposed from the top of it. The sight of this menacing device causes Dr. Levitt to begin a violent struggle with his restraints as the figure picks up two of the black cables, and turns on the machine. The humming noise from the box fills Dr. Levitt's head with horrific thoughts of what is to come.

Dr. Levitt's breathing becomes labored as he continues fighting against the restraints before stopping as his energy level depletes. Dr. Levitt is now hyperventilating his shirt is completely drenched in sweat with terror in his eyes when his captor decides to speak.

"My understanding is that you are a psychiatrist."

Not knowing what is going to happen next and seeing that his captor seems to know a lot about him he feels that lying would not be a smart thing to do. So Dr. Levitt nods nervously as the hooded figure stands placing the cables on top of the bed. It reaches down grabs Dr. Levitt pants leg and rolls it up, then reaches for the cable and attaches it tightly around his ankle.

Dr. Levitt begins to scream begging for his life and freedom.

"My God, what are you going to do?! Please stop. Please! Just let me go and I won't tell anyone!"

Ignoring his pleas the faceless stranger repeats the process on his left ankle. Dr. Levitt fear is at an unprecedented level of frenzy. But then in a moment of clarity he believes that even though he is completely terrified he must think of something to get out of this situation. He believes that maybe trying to reach out to the stranger on a professional level might help.

"Please talk to me. Let me try and help you. Why are you doing this to me?"

But without saying a word, the hooded figure returns to the device and picks up the last two cables, attaching them to each wrist. Dr. Levitt realizes that nothing he does is working, so he returns to the only thing he is able to do.

"Help! I'm in here! Help me!"

All his cries for help fall on death ears as the loud humming noise from the menacing device drown out the sounds of his screams. Dr. Levitt is now completely attached to the device. The figure walks over to the device, picks up a small black box from the side of it and sits on the stool by Dr. Levitt's head.

"So doc have you ever had the need to use electroshock therapy on any of your patients?"

Fearing for his life Dr. Levitt nervously answers immediately. "I would never use that on my patients."

The hooded figure stares at the doctor for a minute then points its gloved hand at the doctor, "Are you telling me the truth doctor?"

"Yes, yes..."

But before he can finish his sentence, a jolt of electricity is shot through his entire body. His back arches up off the stretcher as he trembles and screams in pain. As Dr. Levitt yells out in the agony the hooded figure stands up speaking with anger in its voice yelling over Dr. Levitt's screams.

"If there's one thing I hate, it's liars!"

After what had seemed like an unbearable eternity of pain to Dr. Levitt the electric current is finally shut down, which causes Dr. Levitt's body to drop back down to the bed. He moans and whimpers as his body feels completely numb, his ankles and wrist are burning. He sobs uncontrollably hoping that this is the end of his ungodly torture. In an instant without missing a step the hooded figure demeanor changes and its voice turns back to its original monotone manner.

"Isn't this the method you use to break a person will?" The faceless stranger asks.

Fearing that his hell is far from over he begins to beg for mercy.

"Please, please no more! I have never done this to anyone I swear," he pleads with tears in his eyes.

The only thing that his plea receives is another jolt of electricity being sent through his body, this time causing his body to gyrate uncontrollably. His face begins to turn red and contort in a horrific manner appearing as if it was about to explode from the current flowing through his body,

The room already had a musty smell, which is slowly being converted to a more horrific stench as the electricity that is coursing through Dr. Levitt's body causes him to lose control of his bodily functions. Yellow and brown stains begin to appear on his clothes and on the sheets. The electricity continues racing through Dr. Levitt's body, while the hooded figure stands over him looking down at his tortured face.

"Don't lie to me doctor. Don't you know by now that I know everything you have done?"

Suddenly the pulsating electricity is turned off causing Dr. Levitt's body to stop gyrating. As his body lays there his ankle and wrist have smoke rising from them. A small whiff of burnt flesh begins to resonate throughout the room along with the stench of urine and fecal matter. Dr. Levitt is moaning in pain coughing and sobbing as his tormentor walks back to the stool and sits back down.

Mucus flows freely out Dr. Levitt's nose and saliva is sliding down his cheek pooling on the bed. Dr. Levitt's mouth is moving as he tries to talk through all the pain, attempting to put words together, so he can beg for mercy. After a few minutes he finally has the strength to speak to his tormentor.

"I'm sorry, okay? Please just stop. I'll tell you the truth. You're right I did use it on my patients. I was just doing my job. I was trying to help them. But please, please no more just stop."

The tormentor rises up and walks over to the humming machine and places the small black box on the floor next to it without saying a word. The hooded figure begins to pace around the room slowly with its hands behind its back acting as if it was contemplating its next move before suddenly stopping and turning toward Dr. Levitt.

"So what you are telling me is that you were trying to help people by giving them electroshock therapy. "What a coincidence that's what I'm doing now. Huh, who knew?" Shrugging its shoulders nonchalantly it turns and walks towards the door.

"I'm sorry for whatever I've done! Please let me go. I won't tell anyone. I just want to go home!"

Dr. Levitt screams out in agonizing horror as the steel door slam shut echoing over his screams of terror.

# CHAPTER 12

The hooded figure feeling that each guest had received personal attention from their host walks down a narrow hallway passing by all their rooms. Listening, ignoring the screams and pleas of its guests, it reaches a door that has a bright glow from underneath it. The hooded figure opens the door that leads into a brightly lit room. The brightness in the room is not coming from any windows, but from the flickering of several closed circuit television monitors.

The room is large, appearing to have been an office at some point in time. It appears to have been unused for years as the windows are boarded up and there are several pieces of office furniture strewn throughout. The area where the captor walks toward is in the far corner of the office. It is a makeshift office cubicle with a ragged office chair in the center and the desk crammed against the wall.

There are seven television monitors mounted on a stack of metal shelves, each monitor providing a visual of each one of the guests. There are two monitors that focus on the hallways of the guests and the seventh monitor is completely dark showing no images at all. It pulls the office chair toward the desk and sits down to watch them all. Watching and reveling in their every movement, in their every scream and in every pathetic plea for mercy.

It focuses on each and every one of it guests staring methodically at each screen slowly moving from one screen to the next from its makeshift control room.

After a few minutes of studying all the guests it has finally seen enough and reaches over to the center console and flips up a switch, turning on the internal intercom to all the rooms. The hooded figure has decided it's time that all its guests hear from their host again.

"Hello, my friends. It's me again. I just wanted to make sure that everyone is comfortable and enjoying their accommodations. This place does have a meaning to some of you, but we will get to that later. But now it's time to play: This Is Your Life."

At the exact moment the faceless stranger speaks those last words, the television monitors in every room turn on simultaneously. Deborah is tired, battered and exhausted when the television turns on her reaction to the explicit image of Ariel on the screen. She stands unsteadily trying to stay on her feet using the bed post to limp towards the television. Unable to handle the weight on her injured ankle she collapses to the ground trying to reach out to the image on the television.

"What have you done to my baby?!"

She bawls as she stares at the image of her daughter, who sits unconscious in the chair, her light blue blouse stained and caked in her own blood. Ariel's face is hardly recognizable from the slash marks on her head from the razor which has left a trail of blood down her face.

With some effort, Dr. Levitt manages to raise his head and tries to focus on the new light source that has engulfed his room and sees the image of Ariel. The image of the bloody girl causes him first to scream in terror, but then causes him to start shouting for help praying that he won't end up just like her.

Unlike the others, Det. Gibson is at a disadvantage as he can't see anything and because of what he has already endured, he is barely lucid enough to understand or even hear what was said through the intercom or the television. The faceless figure takes a few more minutes to bask in the pleasure of seeing their reactions to the images or sounds coming from the monitors and before deciding to introduce the party guests to each other.

"So now that everything should start sinking in to you all, it is only right that I introduce everyone just in case you don't recognize each other. First, we have Deborah Garfield formerly known as Deborah Wilson. We also have her lovely and vivacious daughter Ariel, a special child who has followed in her mother's footsteps. We also have Detective Tim Gibson, the best cop money and sex can buy and last, but not certainly not least, Dr. Julius Levitt, whose specialty depends on how much you pay him."

As the words continue through the intercom the image on the television in Dr. Levitt's room has changed. As he recognized the new person on the screen is Deborah, he remembers her and calls out to her hoping she will hear his screams.

"Deborah, I'm here! Please help me!"

He knows that his screams will go unanswered and that Deborah is no position to help, but it is the only thing that he can do to give him some form of hope. Eventually all the excruciating pain that he has endured and his brief outburst cause Dr. Levitt to pass out. Throughout all the speeches and introductions from their captor, Det. Gibson has been in and out of consciousness. Then he hears Deborah's name briefly in his incoherent state and screams out impulsively for her.

"Deborah! I'm here!"

But his one moment of lucidity is brief as he once again goes unconscious from the pain. The hooded figure leans in very close to the intercom and speaking in a meticulous manner. "Today, we will set the record straight. You all will eventually be reborn, but for that to happen, you must first all die."

With one hit of a switch, the intercom and all the monitors turn off simultaneously within the rooms. Deborah sobs uncontrollably as she pushes herself backward to lean against the bed her arms folded across her chest rocking back and forth as she stares up to a blank screen still horrified thinking about the recurring image of her daughter's bloody face. The hooded figure stands and looks at each guest on each monitor before turning them off one at a time then exiting the control room.

# CHAPTER 13

The door to Ariel's room opens allowing the hooded figure to enter the room quietly. Noticing that Ariel is unconscious it decides to let her know that she has company by slamming the door. The sound causes Ariel to awaken in terror looking around the room afraid, when she realizes that standing in the center of the room staring at her is her jailer.

"You look good bald. I can see my reflection on your head." It laughs as it admires its handy work.

Even though Ariel feels the throbbing stinging pain in her scalp her anger is visible through her blood streaked face. She struggles violently against her restraints trying to get loose.

"Calm down, you seem so angry with me. Is there something you want to tell me?"

Her tormentor begins to walk toward her causing Ariel to fear what other torturous pain she was going to have to endure. Instead, without uttering a word, it removes the saliva, blood and mucus covered gag from her mouth letting it drape around her neck. Her mouth now clear of obstruction, she begins to cough clearing her throat. After a few minutes of coughing and spitting out phlegm, she begins to feels an exuberant burst of energy that slowly turns to anger, while looking at her antagonist who is staring at her.

"You motherfucker! Why are you doing this to me?! Who you do fucking think you are? I know people! You are so fucking dead when I get out of here! Do you hear me? Dead!"

Ariel's eyes are red, tears roll down her cheeks as she violently struggles against her restraints during her tirade. The hooded figure stands there motionless, uncaring about her outburst and then suddenly breaks its silence.

"Why did I do this? Don't you remember the pain, betrayal and anguish you caused him?"

Ariel stops her struggling and even though she feels weak, looks toward her abductor with disgust and anger not understanding what was said nor having any idea what this person was speaking about.

"What the fuck are you talking about you sick freak? I have no fucking clue what you're talking ab...?"

Before she's able to complete her sentence the hooded figure steps closer to her chair and smacks her across her face leaving a red welt on her already bloody face. The impact splits her lip causing a mixture of new blood and old to fly off her face.

"You bitch. I'm not surprise you don't remember him, why would you since you betrayed him after he did so much for you?"

Ariel screams in pain as she shakes her head sobbing trying to comprehend why this was happening. After receiving the smack to her face, fear sets in while looking at the hooded figure. She then becomes speechless, afraid that anything she might do or say will cause her to feel its wrath once again. So she sits there silently with the added pain of the smack resonating through her body waiting for its next move and fearing the worst.

Throughout Ariel outburst her captor does nothing except stand there observing her silently, which causes her to feel even more uneasy. Suddenly the hooded figure turns its back to Ariel and slowly raises it hands lowering the heavy black hood down from its head. The removal of the hood allows Ariel for the first time to see black hair from the back of this person's head. It is the first sign that there is an actual person underneath this costume.

The figure slowly removes the mask off its face tossing it aside nonchalantly. Ariel's anxiety is at an all-time high waiting to see who this malevolent being is that has been physically and mentally torturing her. Suddenly the person spins around like a magician that has just performed a spectacular trick.

"Ta-da!"

Ariel gasps in disbelief. This evil person is a woman. She was gorgeous, with jet black shoulder-length hair, piercing blue eyes, a button type nose and small, but voluptuous lips. Her beautiful looks and the fact that she is a woman are not the only thing that is causing Ariel to be in complete shock.

"Hi Sis, I do love your new look," she says with a light laugh.

Ariel is still in complete shock at who was behind the mask this entire time.

"Suzanne!" Ariel shouts, incredulous.

Suzanne places her hands on her hips and smiles at her older sibling.

"Oh my god, you remember me. I'm so touched, but you didn't call, you didn't write." Suzanne responds merrily.

Ariel looks down toward the ground shaking her head, hoping this is all just a bad dream.

"No, no, no, no! This can't be real!"

She glances up looking at her half-sister who is standing there smiling.

"Why are you doing this? What did I ever do to you?"

Suzanne inches closer to Ariel's chair, stopping within inches of her, Suzanne then raises her arms with her fist balled up and placed them next to the edge of her eyes moving them in a back and forth motion mocking Ariel's sobbing.

"Boo Hoo, pity me. This is so like you, give it a rest. All of you are responsible for my father's death."

Ariel leans forward against her restraints.

"What are you talking about? You are fucking crazy."

Suzanne finds her struggles comical as she folds her arms across her chest. She places her right index finger to the side of her head and begins slightly tapping her head acting as if she is deliberating something. Suddenly she stops and drops her arms.

"Um yeah, of course I'm crazy don't you remember? Dear old mom put me in the mental hospital using her connection with Dr. Levitt to get me committed as a paranoid schizophrenic."

Even though she has not seen Suzanne in years, Ariel hopes that she can reason with her, that she can touch her humanity and get Suzanne to show her some compassion.

"Suzanne, you needed help. You were always acting weird; trying to hurt yourself. Seeing and hearing things that weren't happening. Mom was just trying to get you help. I just want to help you now; please just let me help you."

Suzanne stared intently at her listening to every word of Ariel's passionate plea without replying. Suzanne head droops and she turns away from Ariel. Suzanne's reaction gives Ariel a sign of hope that maybe she had reached her.

Suddenly Suzanne's laughter echoes throughout the room. She's bending over holding her sides, feeling like her ribs were going to split in half.

"Oh my God! Wow! Now that was funny. I haven't laughed so hard since I don't know... I shaved your head. She tries to catch her breath from her moment of amusement. "Okay, I'm sorry so let me get this straight you mean keeping me locked in a room was supposed to help me? Where they raped and tortured me and that was supposed to help me? Well, shit when you say it like that it makes sense, now I understand." Suzanne lets out another laugh.

"Since you and mom were trying to help me so much, I want to share a few of my great stories of all the fun I had while I was getting all this help you both were making sure I would receive."

Suzanne walks toward the door and exits the room briefly returning with a chair placing it in front of Ariel. Suzanne takes a seat and swings one leg on top of the other, crossing them while tapping her finger on the side of her head jokingly trying to recall her stories.

"Okay, let me see where do I begin my story? Well the best way to tell a story is always from the beginning, you know, the beginning of my healing process," Suzanne says chuckling.

# CHAPTER 14

"You see ten years ago, our dear old mom decided I was ill and needed help, so she had me institutionalized at the Tremont Mental Hospital. I remember every single thing that happened to me, since it happened to me every night. My room was so very similar to the one you are in right now. I figure the best way for you to understand my story is to have as many props as possible. I wanted to make sure that you get to share my full experience. I wore a dirty white hospital gown. I was kept barefoot and was hardly given the opportunity to wash myself. Eventually by body and hair matched my filthy gown. My hair became matted not only with dirt but after time some of my blood. Aren't you lucky you will never have that problem?"

"Fuck you, you crazy bitch!" Ariel lashes out.

Suzanne stands and leans in close to Ariel's face. "Listen, I'm trying to tell you a story. If you can't be quiet and listen nicely, I will have to gag you again. Now can you please be quiet like a nice little girl?" She strokes Ariel's cheek gently, her black glove getting lightly stained with the remnants of her blood-stained face.

Suzanne's words terrify her as she thinks of what other horrors Suzanne might unleash on her if she feels she is being disrespected so she nods in agreement. Suzanne takes her seat, pauses and then clears her throat before continuing.

"Okay now where was I? Oh yeah the floors were dirty and the light in the room was very dim. I was so cold, afraid in that room and didn't understand why I was there and nobody would tell me anything except that I needed help. Hey, but not to worry because my hero Dr. Levitt was going to make sure people were there to check on me and take care of me. He was such a thoughtful man.

"I wouldn't allow those men to look after a plant, but they worked for Dr. Levitt and god knows what else they did around the hospital. But one of their main functions was to make sure that I was taken care of during my stay. The first guy wasn't a charmer by any stretch of the word. His name was Steve; he was such a pleasant 300lb man with a huge belly. He was balding, had a scruffy beard and wore white hospital scrubs that looked more grayish than white. He also had one of the most unpleasant body odors I had ever smelled and my Lord could he have used a box of breath mints.

"But I'm sorry I digress. Let's me get back to the story. During my entire stay there, they would bring me several pills every day that I had to take three times a day.

"They would make me feel completely lethargic and nauseous, but there was no escaping it; normally a female nurse would be the one to ensure that I would take the pills. So I decided that I would no longer take them, then for whatever reason Steve stated that he would be the one bringing me my pills. On one of these days he saw me throw out my pill, so he took it upon himself to make sure that I took my pills and he tried to force me to open my mouth..."

Suzanne paused and leaned back in the seat, tilting her head up towards the ceiling as she recalls everything, word for word, that happened on that day.

"Steve's large burly body with the horrible body odor and unpleasant breath was on top of me, forcing open my mouth. 'Come on you little bitch open your mouth and take your pills.' He used both his hands to pry my jaw open.

"I tried my hardest to fight him off with all my strength and waited for the opportunity to present itself. He took his fat chubby disgusting fingers and slipped them into my mouth, at that moment I bit down on both of his fingers causing him to howl in pain and release my face. In an instant and without hesitation he slapped me powerfully in the mouth, which caused me to cry and blood to dribble out of my mouth. 'You bitch. John, will you give me a fucking hand?' Steve yelled toward the open room door.

"It was bad enough to have to deal with one goon, but now I had to deal with two of them. The other goon in question was named John. He was a tall, thin, lanky douche bag with long, black, stringy hair that was always pulled back into a ponytail. His body odor was not as bad as his partner, but his clothes could definitely fool you as they were also stained in perspiration and dirt. His crooked smile exposed his stained yellow teeth. 'What's up Steve? You're girlfriend giving you a hard time?'

"I twisted and fought as hard as I could with Steve as John towered over both of us laughing and Steve's chubby fingers still trying to force me to open my mouth so I could take those damn pills. 'Will you hold this bitch down, so I can shove these pills down her throat? But be careful the, bitch bites.' John walked over toward my head, leaned down and grabbed both of my flailing arms, pulling them over my head. He then dropped down to his knees and placed each of my arms under his knees. I could feel the weight of his body on my arms causing extreme pain. I then felt drops of saliva from John's mouth hitting my forehead as he stared down at me with a twisted smile on his face enjoying what is taking place.

"I could see the look of excitement in both of their eyes, that look of pleasure I saw in their face made me angrier causing me to fight even harder. But the harder I fought the more enjoyment they seem to get as John's then used his hands to hold my head still as Steve's hands pulled my legs straight, which allow him to straddle me with all of his ungodly weight across my hips.

"Steve used one hand to pinch my nose shut. I tried to calm myself so that I could hold my breath, but it was impossible because of all the struggling I'd done. So my chest began to tighten. I had no choice but to open my mouth, gasping for air taking in a huge breath. At that opportune moment Steve shoved all the pills down my throat and clamped his hand over my mouth, forcing me to swallow them.

"Once they heard the unbearable gulp, they released me as I gagged and coughed. The both stood, ecstatic about their accomplishment. 'I keep telling little miss thing over here. When you mess with the bull you'll always get the horns.' Steve said as they both chuckled.

"Every night that hideous and unrelenting laugh would replay in my mind over and over again." Suzanne pauses momentarily before continuing with her story.

"When they both left the room I lay on the ground crying in pain. I would eventually have to get used to it because I would cry myself to sleep on many nights; the torture I endured came in different forms every night.

"They were trying to debase me, humiliate me, and break me by treating me like an animal. I finally found the strength to get off the floor and lay on my bed crying until I fell asleep. Then later that night, the sound of the lock on the door awoke me as they re-entered my room with a wheel chair. They were looking at me like I was some sort of meat. 'Hey girly your stench is getting to be a little too ripe to handle. You need to get cleaned up,' Steve said.

"I looked up at him with disgust and rage. But did not say a word, I wanted him to come closer to me until his face was close enough for me to hack up a nice big wad of phlegm onto his face. I knew all I had to do was draw him in by smiling at him, feeding his giant size ego.

"He smiled as he walked toward, leaned in and then bam. It was beautiful, one of my best as it landed right between the big man's eyes. 'Boy you are such a ladies' man,' John said as he laughed uncontrollably. Steve stood there hovering over me with the phlegm dripping down his face.

"I waited and prepared for some form of reprisal a slap across the face, a punch in the stomach or dragging me off the bed by my hair. But what he did next was surprising and disgusting as he casually wiped his face with his hand and licked it cleaning off every bit of phlegm from the palm of his calloused hand. Those actions just confirmed the fact that he was just a disgusting vile pig. 'Mmmm...You are so tasty.'

"I began to slowly regress by body back further into my bed, all of a sudden they lunged toward me furiously grabbing my body off the bed and tossing me into a wheelchair. I tried to fight them off, but it's a losing battle as they quickly won and strapped me into the wheelchair.

"My screams for help didn't bring anyone to the rescue, they never did. The only other sound you heard in my room was the cackling coming from Steve and John. John doubled checked the straps making sure they had me tightly strapped in the wheelchair as he pushed me out of my room and toward the institution's showers with Steve leading the way. 'Now I know why you like her, Steve. She is so feisty.'"

"I started to yell out, but all that got me was a dirty rag that smelled and tasted like putrid water being shoved in my mouth. I gagged immediately and puked into the rag causing me to choke on my own vomit. When they realized what was happening they removed the rag acting as they were doing me a favor at that moment I wished they would had let me die. 'Hey baby, you got to be careful you wouldn't want to die on us. That would get us in a lot of trouble,' Steve said with a laugh.

"Once we arrived in the shower rooms, Steve shut the door behind us. John pushed the wheelchair into the far shower stall, turned the wheelchair around so my back was up against the wall and I was facing them.

Steve walked off into another room returning briefly dragging in a large fire hose.

"Steve lifted the nozzle of the hose and pointed it directly at me. John moved away from Steve and his new found toy. 'Yep my girl is a spitfire; a dirty little spitfire. But we are going to take care of all that.'

"Steve grinned and signaled John to go over to the water main and turn it on. John couldn't return fast enough to enjoy the show, when he heard a blast of water from the shower stall. When he returned he saw the cold arctic blast of water hitting me in the face feeling like miniature knife stabbing my face simultaneously. I was unable to scream as every time I open my mouth, I swallowed more and more water, even when I kept my mouth closed it was almost impossible to breathe due to the amount of water being blasted at me.

"But even through all the noise of the rushing water, I could faintly make out those two bastards laughing at my expense. Even if they did hear my cries I knew they wouldn't stop their water game; they were enjoying it too much. My body began to convulse from the freezing water, I was finding it harder and harder to breathe wishing that they would had let me choke on my own vomit. 'Hey, Stevie boy, make sure you don't forget to wash her ass!' John said, still laughing hysterically.

"After what felt like an eternity, the water was finally turned off as I begin to cough and spit up all the water that had filled my lungs even vomiting some of the water. I thought that my ordeal for this night had come to an end, but it was far from over. Steve dropped the hose on the ground, walked over toward me and begins grabbing my hair as I'm still coughing trying to get all the water out of my lungs. 'Okay, now we need to do something about this hair.' Steve left the room briefly, while John was busy rolling up the hose and dragging it away.

"Steve returned acting very suspicious with both his hands behind his back. When John re-entered the room he looked over at his friend, curious as to what he was up to. 'So what you got there buddy?' John asked.

"Steve brought his hands forward exposing the secret item he was hiding behind his back—a pair of hair clippers. Steve methodically walked towards my shivering, cold and beaten body. 'I think I have a way to make sure she stops having bad hair days.' Steve turned on the clippers; the buzzing noise emanating from the clippers briefly made me forget the burning feeling in my throat from all the water I had swallowed. I screamed to him, begged him to stop and not do this to me.

"My words had no merit, Steve ignored my words, completely fixated on my hair as the humming sound of the clippers got louder the closer they got to my head. As if at that exact moment I had been transported into a time warp causing time to slow down. Everything I felt from that moment forward was happening at a snail's pace. I felt the clippers slowly moving along my head scrapping against my scalp cutting off my hair. I cried and whimpered quietly as pieces of my hair fell all around me. For the first time since being placed in that hell-hole I felt helpless, defeated with no fight left. 'Stop whining. This is a better look for you. Don't you want to look your best for our date later?' Steve remarked with a smile.

"The more I cried the more enjoyment it seemed to give Steve. A few times during my ordeal he would pick up a few pieces of my cut strands of hair and toss them up in to the air just like you would confetti on New Year's.

"As soon as he was finally done cutting almost every piece of hair that he could John and him stood back staring at me admiring his work, commenting as if he had just created a work of art by mutilating my head.

"They stood there for a few minutes laughing and mimicking my torment. Once they had their fill of gratification, John wheeled me back to my room or as I like to call it to my hell. Once back in my room, Steve did not waste any time undoing my straps, then lifted me out of the wheelchair and tossed me on to my cold dirty mattress.

"I laid there afraid and exhausted not saying a word. I was cold and my body was shaking uncontrollably, wishing this night would finally come to an end. In my current state my vision was blurry and unfocused as I gazed up noticing Steve whispering into John's ear. Whatever he told John put a smile on his face, as John turned toward the door. I was confused not understanding what was going until I saw Steve's chubby face grinning as he sauntered toward my bed.

"I began to drag my body away from him, as I tried to focus on what he was doing with his hands. That's when I noticed him untying the drawstring from his dirty hospital scrubs. 'Hey, don't wear her out. Don't forget she has another date later tonight,' John said as he closed the door, trapping my screams in that room.

"Like any other day or night, my screams for help went unanswered and blended into the darkness." Suzanne says as she stands up from her chair.

The entire time Suzanne was telling her story Ariel had been staring at Suzanne hoping that recalling these horrific memories would make her easier to talk to if she spoke to her compassionately.

"Oh my God, Suzanne I'm sorry that happen to you, but I didn't know. You have to believe me I had nothing to do with any of that. That's why I don't understand why you are taking it out on me."

Suzanne shakes her head as she looks over at Ariel.

"You know what is really so sad is that you are still unwilling to take responsibility for your actions. But you see every cloud has a silver lining and something good did come out of me being at the hospital. While I was there I found out the truth."

Ariel attempts to follow Suzanne as she begins to pace and circle her chair.

"Okay now what was I talking about? Sometimes we crazy people lose our train of thought," Suzanne says as she pauses briefly before continuing her pacing.

"Oh yeah right, the good that came out of being in the hospital. You see any time I heard that sliding lock I became numb. I tried to put my mind somewhere to help me get over the abuse I was about to endure. But on one particular night everything changed for me. On this night, when the door opened the person that walked in wasn't there to hurt me."

# CHAPTER 15

Suzanne pauses for a minute as she recalls the night that saved her life, thinking about the day she met the man that would answer so many of her questions. "The man who entered the room that night was not there to hurt me, he was there to help me his name was Michael and he knew my father. You have to understand when he first came into the room, my first reaction was to retreat fearing that this man was going abuse me as the others did. I didn't believe for a minute that he was a friend of my father, but he showed me a picture of my father as a teenager standing next to a younger version of the man that was standing in front of me.

"I kept staring at the picture of my father rubbing my fingers over my father image remembering the good times we spent together, as tears began rolling down my face. I missed him so much. The stranger's words brought me back to reality. 'Suzanne, listen, I don't have much time. I came here to try and help you.'

"I asked him where my father was. Michael quickly walked over and took a seat at the edge of my bed. He held his index finger up to his lips, encouraging me to lower me voice. 'Suzanne, please you must be quiet and listen very carefully. I don't know how to tell you this but your dad is dead."

"I couldn't believe his words and began lashing out at him, tears flowing down my face profusely as my rage took over. I accused him of lying and that my father was not dead. Michael tried to console me, make me see reason so he could explain to me what happened.

'Suzanne I know this is hard for you to hear, but you must listen to me. Before he died, your father left something for you in my possession. I couldn't bring it to you here, because I knew they would take it from you. So the minute you are released, you have to come see me. I will give you the package. I promised your father that I would do everything I can to help you and believe me I will."

"I was still crying when Michael reached for my trembling hand to comfort me and instead of accepting his gracious act I push myself further away deeper into the dark corner of my bed. 'Suzanne please you must listen, I don't have much time. Do you understand what I've just told you?' He looked over his shoulder toward the door every few seconds in fear of someone walking in and being discovered. I quickly wiped the tears from my eyes and slid myself toward him and looked into his eyes. I asked him if my father died in prison.

"He hesitated and then briefly glanced towards the door once again before turning back to answer me. 'No, he was out of jail on probation, but he was being harassed by someone after he got out. He wouldn't tell me who was doing this to him, but I have an idea who was behind his harassment. When he found out you were being kept in here, he tried to get you out, but he wasn't allowed to contact you and not being able to help really send him into a downward spiral of depression then, um...He committed suicide.'

"I noticed that he was really hurt by my father death, which brought me to the conclusion that this man really cared about my father. Feeling more trust for this man I sat even closer to him. I asked him who the person was harassing my father and how could he help me. 'Listen, Suzanne I will tell you everything once you are out but for now listen. You will be turning 18 in three weeks and you will no longer be considered a juvenile. Your mother will no longer have any say on your stay here as long we can prove that you are not a danger to yourself or anyone else.'

"When he said those words I started to doubt this man's intentions and thought it was all just another false promise from someone who didn't care about me. I told him they lied when they had me committed and they would lie to keep me from being released. They couldn't afford to release me because I knew the truth about what happened to my father. My mother didn't want me out of there.

"I pushed myself back to the far edge of the bed once again, but this time Michael followed me, determined to win me over. 'I understand your frustration Suzanne, but you must believe me and trust me, I promised your father and I'm promising you I will get you out of here. Just remember your father left you a package along with money—a large sum of money in fact. He had been saving money for you from the day you were born. Your own mother doesn't know about the money he stashed away for you.'

"The more he spoke the more I began to believe again, he finally convinced me that he was there to help me. 'I have already hired you an attorney, he has already begun working on your paper work and once you turn 18 you will be released. Upon your release the attorney will give you my address, once you come see I will give you everything. I must leave now, but we will see each other again I promise.'

"Michael patted my leg to reassure me that everything will be okay, slid down to the edge of the bed and stood. I couldn't resist as I jumped off the bed gave him a big hug and whispered a thank you into his ear. He smiled and it was the first sign of kindness I had in a long time. It was a quick hug, but it buoyed up my spirits as I watched him leave."

Suzanne glances over at Ariel and notices the she isn't showing an ounce of interest in what she had been saying even avoiding eye contact with her.

Suzanne strolls over to Ariel surprising her and squeezes her cheek with her right hand, turning her attention where it should be focused—on her.

"So you see dear old sister, I had to endure all this hell because of dear old mom. During those years, I wanted to die every day, but when I learned what my father had endured, I started to get angry and all the anger I had toward all of you kept me going every day." Anger and disdain tinged Suzanne's voice.

Ariel begins to beg to Suzanne.

"I'm sorry, all that happen to you, but I didn't know about any of this, I told you before I had nothing to do with any of those things."

Suzanne squeezes Ariel cheeks tighter with her forefinger and thumb, which cause Ariel to shriek in pain. After a few minutes she releases her face forcefully pushing her head backwards making the back of her head smack into the head rest, she then begins to pace around the room once again.

"How dare you say you had nothing to do with this? Were you not listening, all of you are responsible. You all are responsible for my father's death."

Suzanne continues her tirade, until Ariel's sudden outburst causes Suzanne to pause.

"I didn't make your father commit suicide!"

Suzanne freezes, turns toward Ariel and slapped her across the face again.

The impact leaves a bigger red welt through her already bloody and bruised face. The impact brings more crying from Ariel as Suzanne bites her bottom lip and stares ominously at Ariel.

"You bitch! After all you and dear old mom did to him; you destroyed his business, you destroyed his character, making him feel like trash, like an animal. I'm going to make sure that you get to know exactly how he felt." Suzanne walks toward the exit, she opens the door and is about to step out of the room.

Ariel feeling completely unrepentant after hearing Suzanne disturbing tales of pain and suffering lashes out toward her spitefully.

"I never like you or your father! I'm happy mom put you in that hospital! You are just mad because you and your father are both fucking losers and you both deserved everything that happened to you!"

Suzanne's hand slides off the door knob, pushes the door close and stares at the ground without responding to the venomous outburst coming from Ariel. Suddenly Suzanne turns around, glaring over at Ariel whose hateful words ringing are in her ears. At that exact moment Ariel knows that she has made a mistake and those words would come back to haunt her.

"Stay away from me! I'm sorry. I didn't mean it!"

Suzanne's eyes don't shift away from Ariel's. Ariel attempts to push her body away the closer Suzanne gets, but the restraints prevent this from happening. Suzanne leans over as Ariel turns her face away cringing, as Suzanne whispers hoarsely into her ear.

"You know when we were growing up I always thought you talked too much. Let's see if I can't do something to fix that problem."

Suzanne reaches into the oversize pocket of her robe and pulls out a small shiny black box bring in towards Ariel face. Ariel terrified to look at Suzanne directly glances over to see the shiny black box without making eye contact with her.

"What is in that box?" Ariel asks nervously.

Suzanne opens the black box and removes an item that brings a chill up Ariel spine, filling her eyes with panic. Ariel begins to scream violently, futilely struggling against her restraints, as Suzanne smiles at her without saying a word. Suzanne enjoys the terror she sees as she goes in toward Ariel face straddling her body with her new toy in hand. Ariel is screaming and her feet are thrashing around in their straps, but after a few seconds her screams stop as do her movements.

After a few minutes Suzanne dismounts and steps back away from Ariel staring at her, she places her right index finger against her lips lightly.

"Shhhhhh…"

Suzanne begins walking to the door. Before exiting, she turns toward Ariel, a smile touching her lips.

# CHAPTER 16

D r. Levitt is slowly coming to, getting his grip back on reality and soon feels a deep, burning sensation around his joints. The pain is a throbbing and painful reminder that he is still being held prisoner in his own private hell.

"Oh dear God please help me. This cannot be happening to me. Let this be a bad dream." He moans, restlessly and slowly moving his head from side to side.

That is when he hears that dreadful, familiar sound of the slide lock opening confirming to him that this is not a dream. The door opens and Suzanne parades into the room no longer wearing the mask or hooded robe. Instead she is wearing a casual pair of jeans, a long-sleeved tee carrying a very small black duffle bag. Dr. Levitt immediately sighs in relief, thankful that it is not his captor who entered, but an angel of mercy who is about to free him from this hell.

"Oh my God, you heard my screams! Please you must hurry. Get me out of this before he returns." Dr. Levitt says terrified.

But Suzanne says nothing, she strolls near the edge of the stretcher and stares down at him, smiling; finding pure amusement in his false sense of security. She drags over the stool that she left there from her previous visit placing it next to the stretcher. She plops down on it, dropping the bag on the ground next to her.

"So this guy's crazy huh? What does he look like?" she inquires, trying to keep her composure so she won't burst out laughing.

His nerves are at an all-time high as he turns his head every few moments looking toward the door fearing that the hooded man will not return.

"Please you don't understand, you must hurry, he did this to me. He has been torturing me and others. He is wearing a black hooded outfit with a black mask. We must get out of here before he returns so please hurry and get me out of this."

Without hesitation, Suzanne leans down and reaches into the bag by her feet.

"You mean a mask like this?" She says as she lifts the black mesh mask out of the bag.

Holding it up, showing it to Dr. Levitt as his eyes widen in horror as he stares at it.

"Dear God, it's been you all this time. You are the one that been doing this to me? Why...who are you?"

Suzanne stands dropping her mask on his frail chest as she begins pacing around the room while speaking to him.

"What a shocker that you don't recognize me, but then why would you? You've always turned a blind eye, when they were torturing me. You just gave them their orders. You didn't care what they did to me."

Dr. Levitt's eyes cautiously follow Suzanne constant pacing, confused and terrified by her words. Without fully understanding what she was talking about, he thought he could come up with some consoling words that he hope would save his life.

"Listen I'm so sorry for whatever happened to you, maybe you have me mistaken with someone else. I promise that if you let me go, I can still help you. I am a doctor."

She pauses briefly and glares over at him.

"Wow you are so original," she lets out a light laugh. She then begins to mock him. "It's not me you got the wrong guy. I can help you, I'm a doctor." Suzanne continues laughing then stops abruptly. "You are all such ass clowns." She shakes her head in disbelief.

Suzanne exits the room, briefly mumbling to herself. "Why are they so much in denial?"

Dr. Levitt raises his head toward a squeaking sound of wheels coming from outside the door echoing as the noise keeps getting louder as it gets closer. Suddenly he sees that the squeaking wheels belong to a cart being pushed into the room covered by a white sheet. Whatever is under the sheet is being placed in front of his stretcher. Suzanne removes the sheet exposing a metal cart. Dr. Levitt can't see what is on top of the metal cart, but it appears she is organizing something on top of it. Dr. Levitt is completely confused, but he knows he has to get her to talk to him.

"Listen I'm telling you the truth, I swear. I don't know you. Were you a patient of mine?"

When she hears his question Suzanne stops organizing the contents on top of the tray and her eyes light up like someone just flicked on a light switch. She looks up and starts jumping up and down while clapping her hands.

"Ding, ding, ding! We've got a winner, Johnny!"

He squints and cranes his neck hoping that it will help him identify this stranger. But no matter how hard he squints, her face is still foreign to him. Knowing that she is a former patient his mind desperately races to remember her name.

"Okay. So you were a patient. Tell me your name so I can help you," he says in a soft voice.

Ignoring his words she walks around him and begins to remove the cables that are connected to his wrists and ankles. Dr. Levitt sighs in relief, his mind at ease believing that his ordeal is finally over and he is about to be released. He believed that his words of kindness gave her the positive attention she was looking from someone and believed he was going to help her. He was counting on her trusting him, but once she released his restraint he planned to jump out of the bed and run far from this place.

When she removes the last cable from his joints, he realizes that she did not loosen the restraints as she returns to her seat.

"You know what Doc? I was thinking instead of me telling you my name, let me tell you a short story and see if you can guess. It will be more informative, more fun," She says.

Dr. Levitt blankly stares at her, unsure of what to think at this very moment.

"You seem so confused Doc. Don't worry when I finish my story it will all come back to you. But if anything I say sounds familiar and you want me to stop just raise your hand."

"You see once upon a time there was this thirteen year old girl who was forcefully admitted into your hospital by her loving mother. This loving mother claimed that her child was a paranoid schizophrenic. Now a regular doctor would have performed its own test to make its own evaluation, but not you. Instead you asked her a few questions and kept her locked in a room forcing pills down her throat."

With every passing word Dr. Levitt becomes more and more afraid not because he can't remember, but of what she will do if he doesn't.

"Please young lady, if you just tell me who you are I promise I will do my best to help you."

Suzanne looks at him raising her right index finger wagging it back and forth.

"C'mon doc, really what's the fun in that? Now why don't you lay back and relax? Oh, that right you are already laying back. So then let's get back to the story of the young girl and the doctor."

Suzanne begins to tell of the day she met Dr. Levitt.

"I clearly thought that you were a nice man who was going to try and help me during that first meeting. But eventually I would find out the truth. Not just about you, but I would learn the truth about someone else. It ended up being a very important day with a valuable lesson. After everything I went through on that day, I promised myself that I would never make the same mistake twice.

"You introduced yourself and asked if it was okay to ask a few questions. You looked like any doctor one would see on any soap opera or television show. You were wearing a long white lab coat, an ugly tie and khaki pants and you were sitting in a chair next to my bed. The room was brightly lit with no decorations just plain white walls, a bed bolted to the floor and a small table bolted to the floor next to the bed. I guess this was the sample room to make you feel relaxed and make your loved ones think that you are staying in a great place that will help you. But after your initial consult you get shipped off to hotel hell which is the complete opposite of that first room.

"I sat in front of you on the bed an innocent young girl with freckles, silky short black hair and blue eyes. I was extremely nervous and was hoping I could just go home. I asked if after answering your questions I could go home. I began to weep silently feeling confused about the situation I was put in unsure why I was here. 'Well, first answer these few questions then I'll see what I can do about you going home, I promise. So, why do you think you are here?" You asked me in a very soft voice. I responded meekly shrugging my shoulders. 'Did you do anything or say anything that might make someone think you would hurt yourself?' You asked.

"I shook my head furiously from side to side visibly upset by the question. I began twirling a loose strand of my hair. You studied my behavior constantly changing the types of questions you were asking me.

'What about your father? How did he treat you?' You asked.

"The minute I heard that questioned I immediately pushed myself back on the bed leaning up against the wall and pulled my knees into my chest. 'Is something wrong?' You asked as you reached out to touch me. I told you that my father was in jail. That he did nothing wrong and that they all lied! And I began to cry. You asked who lied like you didn't know already.

"Before I could answer that question, our conversation was interrupted by a sudden knock on the door. You walked up and twisted the iron knob to reveal my mother standing in the doorway. She ignored me, acting as if I was not even present in the room. She whispered something in your ear and then you both shook hands."

Suzanne leans forward in the stool and smacks her knee. The noise jolts Dr. Levitt causing him to shriek like a little girl.

"Does any part of this story beginning to sound familiar, does it ring a bell yet?" Suzanne asks.

Some of the story is starting to sound familiar to Dr. Levitt. As he is about to answer her question Suzanne places her index finger to her lips signaling him not speak.

"Hold on, don't answer yet, we are not going to have any spoiler alerts, we are getting to the good part." Suzanne says with a chuckle. She grabs her throat as she clears her it, before continuing. "Where was I? Ah yes now I remember."

"So after my mother and you shake hands, my mother finally looks over at me, while holding a tissue dabbing the corner of her eye with it and I became enraged.

'I appreciate all you're doing for my daughter, Dr. Levitt. I'm so worry about her. She is so disturbed and now she is making up lavish stories.'

"All the anger I felt at her hypocrisy came flowing out and I screamed that I heard about the plan to have my father arrested and about putting stuff in my underwear so it would seem that he did something to me! You and my mother were taken aback by my tirade.

86

'Do you see what I told you doctor? She is in denial to what her father did. I just don't know what else to do with her.'

"Her performance continued with her putting her face in her hands. You attempted to console her, rubbing her shoulders and patting her back. She told you she thought I might hurt myself or someone else and asked for your help, all the while dabbing at her crocodile tears. You sighed pathetically and wrapped your thin arms around my mother's shoulders continuing to pat her back as I looked on in disgust at the sight of this comical charade being orchestrated by my mother.

You told her, 'Don't you worry; I know how much you care for your daughter. We will take very good care of her here. She will be a different person when she leaves here you have nothing to worry about, I will supervise her treatment personally and make sure we don't rush her treatment.'

"My blood was boiling as I could not believe what I was hearing. I knew I could not sit idly by and let my mother destroy my life and my father's. I yelled that there was nothing wrong with me and that I wanted to go home. I tried to run out of the room.

"When I almost got out of there you screamed for help. That's when I first met your goons John and Steve. They rushed into the room, roughly put me into a chair and strapped me down. While I struggled, I glanced over at my mother and instead of wiping away the fake tears; she was smirking—enjoying my predicament.

'You're a sick young girl, but don't worry, we will take care of you,' you said.

"Those two goons of yours backed away and allowed you to lean down inches away from my face to speak to me. At that moment I clear my throat bringing up a large phlegm ball and spit it right in your face and yelled that you were a liar, you were with my mother and that I hated you all.

"You backed away in disgust, grabbing a handkerchief to wipe your face. My mother takes this opportunity to lean in placing her overly glossed lips next to my right ear and whispered the most beautiful words to me.

'You are never getting out of here you little bitch. You tried to ruin everything just like your father tried to do. Your father tried to take everything from me so now I'm taking everything from him. Your father is rotting in prison the same way you are going to rot in here and even that mangy dog of yours that you loved so dearly will be eating its last meal. Good bye, princess.'

"Before my mother backed away she kissed me on the forehead. Her glossy lips left their lip prints on me. I cringed at the feel of my mother's lips on my skin. My mother continued her motherly charade when she noticed you were looking in her direction.

"I glared at both of you as my mother walked out of the room, now I know that you were helping her to keep me in this hell. If you were involved in this from the beginning by helping my mother frame my father, I hope it was worth whatever she gave you. If you weren't involved from the beginning, then you just didn't care what happen to me, either way you are responsible and just as guilty as they are.

"There were countless days and nights that I could see you watching from a distance, never doing anything to help me. So even though you never physically participated in the abuse or laughed along with them, you never tried to stop them. You allowed those two vultures to defile me, so that make you guilty by association."

# CHAPTER 17

Suzanne stood up from the stool walked over toward the farthest wall leaning against it smiling at Dr. Levitt.

"So did you like my story doc? It had everything drama, action, right? Oh it's ok, don't worry. My story does have a happy ending. Now, do you remember my name?"

Dr. Levitt raises his head meekly shaking his head, before it drops back onto the bed not having the strength to hold it up.

"Oh, dear God, yes, yes I remember. You are Deborah Garfield's daughter, Suzanne. But please Suzanne you need to listen to me. You are really sick. What I was doing back then was helping you and if you give me the chance I can still help you now. You just need to release me."

The sudden burst of laughter startles him as he sees her walk over to the foot of the bed.

"Why do you feel the need to lie to me? Have you not learned anything by now? That I'm asking you questions that I already know the answer to."

Suzanne leans down and begins to caress his face, taking some tissues out of her pocket. She uses them to wipe his nose, eyes and mouth, and then tosses the tissues on the floor. He squeezes his eyes shut inhaling, both fearing and hoping that this would just end. But he knows the reality that he will more than likely have to endure more pain and torture, unless he tells her what she wants to hear.

"If I tell you the truth will you please let me go?"

He knows that pleading has not worked for him up to this point, but he hopes that honesty would earn him his freedom. Suzanne finds his comments amusing; she is very curious to hear his version of the truth.

"Okay, but first answer my question then I'll see what I can do about letting you go. I promise, cross my heart and… well you know the rest."

He squeezes his eyes tight again; when he reopens them he looks off into the distance afraid to make eye contact with Suzanne.

"Okay, um… I met your mother one night when she approached me at the Aura Lounge; I used to go there for a drink after work to relax. She approached me and told me she needed my help with a problem. I had no idea who she was or how she knew I was a doctor. I told her I couldn't help her and continued drinking. That's when she …" Dr. Levitt pauses briefly.

"Hey, c'mon doc the story getting interesting," Suzanne says impatiently.

Dr. Levitt continues his story pausing briefly from time to time.

"Your mother's demeanor turned nasty, she leaned into me and told me she knew about all about my gambling debts. She knew I was in severe need of money because the people I owed money didn't like to be kept waiting and I was already late two days. I told them I would have their money by the end of the week. I had no idea how she knew all about my debts, but she had my attention.

"She told me she needed to have her daughter committed into my hospital no questions asked. She told me she needed this done by the next day, I told her that was going to be very hard. But she once again reminded me that it would be in my best interest to do this and she would give me all the money to pay off my debts." Dr. Levitt pauses as tears begin to slowly roll down his cheek as for the first time I think he pondered his actions.

"I was in dire need of financial help and had no choice, but to accept her offer. So the next morning we met, she brought me the money and she gave me all the information I needed to file your commitment papers."

Tears were flowing freely wetting the mattress around his head. Dr. Levitt at no point throughout his story never tried to meet her eyes as his guilt had begun to consume him.

"So you were afraid, huh? You were afraid of what those big bad men would do to you. How are you feeling now, better or worse? Did it ever occur to you that I was afraid? Did it look to you that I enjoyed being brutalized by those men as you watched it happen? They raped me as you watched and you did nothing to stop them, did you enjoy seeing my suffering?"

As Suzanne speaks she begins to slow her words as a thought begins to cross her mind. It causes her to stop talking as she comes to an obvious conclusion that didn't resonate in her mind until now.

"That was part of your agreement with her, wasn't it?" she asks raising her voice.

Dr. Levitt doesn't respond.

"Answer me you piece of shit! Was that part of your agreement?!"

He began crying hysterically, afraid to answer her questions knowing that everything he had done was all catching up to him. The walls were closing in on him.

"I know what I did was wrong and I'm sorry for that, but I never touched you. You know that I never touched you, it was those men. Please forgive me, I'm so sorry. Oh my God! I'm so sorry!"

She grabs the stool and places it against the stone wall and walks over to the metal tray that she had placed by the stretcher earlier, focusing on the contents on the tray. She begins moving around the contents of the tray, Dr. Levitt's view is blocked and due to his weakened state it's hard for him to lift his head up and keep it up long enough to make out what she is doing.

"You're right doctor . . . you never touched me, but you never helped me either. You didn't even care enough to find out, why my mother wanted me committed. All you cared about was saving your own ass."

"That's not true! I tried to help you, but..." Dr. Levitt's voice trails off.

"But what? Let me guess. I was so fucked up in the head that you thought that fucking therapy might work? You enjoyed watching everything they did to me didn't you? So in honor of that, I have a surprise for you."

Suzanne reaches down underneath the bed and pushes a small red button that causes the bed to spring up in one quick jolting motion putting him in an uncomfortable upright sitting position. The jolt causes Dr. Levitt's entire body to jerk forward and he hoped that the sudden jolt might have given him enough leverage to loosen his restraints. But to his chagrin the restraints have not loosened, but the constant jerking motion has caused small little cuts along his wrist and ankles.

Suzanne steps away from the stretcher skipping and humming out of the room briefly. Once again like earlier the squeaky noise of wheels turning are getting louder as they come closer to the room. Dr. Levitt now in a sitting position turns his head toward the sound, when he sees a large rectangular mirror mounted in a brown and black wooden frame attached to the front of a metal cart being pushed in by Suzanne.

She maneuvers the mirror in front of the stretcher, positioning it so Dr. Levitt can see himself. Suzanne walks behind him leaning in so her head is right near his shoulder leaning into his ear as his body quivers seeing the reflection of her face in the mirror smiling next to his own.

She winks at him, making him feel completely vulnerable, and then leans in gives him a kiss on the cheek and whispers into his right ear.

"Since I know that you love to watch, I'm going to make sure that you have the best seat in the house so you won't miss a thing. But let me make sure."

With those ominous words being spoken, Suzanne goes into the black bag and pulls out a leather strap and secures Dr. Levitt's head to the stretcher completely restricting his head movement.

Dr. Levitt begs profusely for mercy, but Suzanne is too busy to acknowledge anything he has to say. She reaches into her pocket and pulls out a metal item that looks like a smaller version of a salad tongs. It has a small twist knob at the top; each end of the tong is rounded and bent inward. Suzanne begins to twist the knob, which causes the tongs to expand.

Dr. Levitt yells for help as she holds this device in her left hand, while taking her right index finger and thumb to open his right eye wide as she brings the device toward his eye.

"Suzanne no! For the love of God, no! Please!"

Suzanne then hooks the tongs to the upper and lower eye lid and begins twisting the knob, which causes the tongs to open exposing his eye by opening the lids wider; Dr. Levitt lets out a blood curdling scream.

His screams do nothing to make Suzanne stop or even hesitate as she pulls out another similar device and repeats the same procedure on his left eye. Once she has finished her work, she stands back to admire her work briefly. Suzanne reaches over to the tray and grabs a long shiny scalpel and walks around behind Dr. Levitt. She holds the scalpel next to him and even with the poor lighting in the room, the scalpel shiny exterior shimmers in the mirror. Dr. Levitt begins violently tugging at his restraints screaming as he sees Suzanne waving the scalpel in the mirror making his heart beat wildly inside his chest.

Dr. Levitt looks down; avoiding her reflection in the mirror, fearing the worst is yet to come. Suzanne begins to feel slighted that he is looking down ignoring her, so she places her cheek tightly against his. She stares at their reflection in the mirror, enjoying what she sees.

"Why are you looking down, this is a very special moment and you need to cherish it. So aren't you lucky I gave you the best seat in the house and the last thing you get to see is my beautiful face?" She lets out a vindictive-laced laugh.

She grabs his head with her left hand and digs the scalpel deep into the bottom of his eye causing a loud horrific scream of agony as a stream of blood splatters onto the mirror. In less than a minute she looks down at her blood drenched hand as she is holding an eyeball in her hand. Dr. Levitt has passed out from the pain and the blood flows down his face and the front of his shirt.

With the eyeball in her hand, she begins to laugh uncontrollably as she looks at his current state. But she knows there is still so much to do that she can't waste time just with him. She begins to smack his face slightly trying to wake him from his unconscious state, slowly he mulls around raising his head, when he sees his bloody image in the mirror seeing a hole where his right eye was causes him to let out a blood-curdling scream.

"What have you done to me?!"

Suzanne giggles excitedly as she feels jubilation.

"I just thought since you love to watch, I didn't want you to miss the grand finale when I cut out your other eye you fucking prick!"

With her final words and scalpel in hand he screams, he goes behind. He screams as even more blood is splashed across the mirror. The horrific screams are followed by an uneasy and unnerving stillness that takes over the room. Suzanne backs away from him and leaves the room.

# CHAPTER 18

Det. Gibson has been in and out of consciousness and feeling gut wrenching pain, still blind to his surroundings and still confused as to the reason why he was being tortured. The only reality he knows is that he strapped to a chair and had his ears cut off by a person who wants him to feel pain with no means of escape. He is fading once again close to losing consciousness, when he hears a noise.

He turns his head weakly toward the sound.

"Hi, Tim. You miss me?"

In his weakened state, he realizes that the person speaking to him is a female, not the person who tortured him and cut off his ears. He tries to focus on the sound of her voice, to make sense of what is going on and what she has to do with all that is going on.

"Please release me. I need medical attention."

When he doesn't hear a response or a sound of any kind, he continues trying to find answers, any type of answers,

"Who are you, lady? Why don't you help? Can you at least tell me your name?"

She doesn't find the need or desire to answer him right away and strolls around his chair stopping briefly behind him, rubbing the leather cushion of the chair. She decides to play a game to torment him further and starts tapping different parts of the chair. The constant tapping around the chair puts him in an agitated state as he moves his head in all directions trying to follow the annoying tapping sound.

Suzanne is enjoying seeing him as his head moves frantically from side to side trying to follow the noise looking like a bloody bobble head. She is in no hurry and is relishing every minute she spends with him. After tormenting him for fifteen minutes with silence, just the small tapping noise around his chair, she decides it's time to answer his questions.

"You see, Det. Gibson the reason I know your name is because we both know some of the same people."

He tries to block the unmerciful pain he feels from his injuries. He knows he needs to try and focus, get his thoughts together, so he can deal with the people who are holding him prisoner.

"Listen, I don't know who you or your friend is, but if he didn't tell you I'm going to fill you in, I'm a cop! You and your partner are in enough trouble, so make it easier on yourself and get me the fuck out of this," he commands.

"Timmy, that was so cute. I like it when you're mad, but you know I can't do that," she responds, coyly.

"What do you mean you can't? Who are you?"

Suzanne decided it's finally time to let him see everything he has been missing. She removes his blind fold, dropping it to the floor then coming out from behind the chair and skipping over to the far wall, leaning up against it.

Det. Gibson eyes automatically begin to squint even though there is hardly any light to cause him any discomfort. Nevertheless due to the amount of time he had been wearing the blindfold his eyesight took a moment to adjust. His eyes flutter until finally his eyes begin to focus on a blurry figure standing against the far wall.

He is forcing his vision to focus on the shadowy figure until he begins to distinguish that the figure is that of a beautiful young woman. She's wearing a blue zip up jacket, a red t-shirt and black jeans. He stares at her completely baffled who is this person and her role in everything that has been going on.

Suzanne's demeanor has changed from how she behaved around her other guests. Instead, she is acting like that quiet shy young girl from those years gone past biting the tip of her nails and awkwardly twisting her body from side to side. She looks up from her nail biting and raised her left hand waving it excitedly at Det. Gibson as if he is a long lost friend that hasn't seen each other in years.

"Hi Timmy, how are you? It has been so long."

His eyes narrow in on her face trying to place this woman who apparently knows him, but her face doesn't resonate with him at all. The cheerful manner that this stranger has addressed him while seeing his current state causes his anger to build up once again. The burning dryness in his throat makes it hard to speak. But he swallows the little bit of saliva he can muster trying to hydrate his mouth before lashing out.

"Where the hell did you come from? How do you know my name?!"

She says nothing. The lack of response from her just infuriates him even more, but he doesn't yell anymore he just stares at her until she finally decides to break her silence.

"Tim, I just don't understand. I was so nice to you when nobody came to your aid. Don't you remember the day in front of Carlos's Bodega and your hand started burning. After I helped you that day this is how you treat me." A huge grin spreads across her face.

Det. Gibson's ire causes his face to turn red, so red that his face becomes brighter than the blood stains on his face.

"That was you?! You did that to me, you crazy bitch?! You are the one responsible for all this!"

His anger doesn't faze her demeanor at all; instead it seems to inspire her. She steps out of the room briefly and brings in a chair, placing it in front of him.

She sits down crossing her legs and places both hands behind her head. She takes a deep breath.

"Oh…Timmy, Timmy, Timmy, do I have one hell of story for you," she beams at him in delight.

Her smugness brings out more rage from Det. Gibson as he begins to writhe against his restrains.

"I don't want to hear any shit from you, you psychotic bitch! The only thing you need to do is untie these straps right now!"

She shakes her head disapprovingly; laughing at the audacity that he has making demands from her given his current condition.

"Tsk…Tsk…Tsk so demanding for a guy that's all tied up. You don't seem to understand, I'm trying to give you what you want. You asked me two questions and I'm going to answer them both, but first I have a little story to tell you. You'll like it believe me."

The areas of his body that have been tied down with restraints are beginning to bleed as the straps have begun to dig into his flesh, due to his battle to release himself from them. But no matter how fierce the anger he displays is, his already weakened body just grows weaker. Suzanne sits, surveying his latest temper tantrum, folding her arms across her chest admiring his determination to free himself.

"I have all day, Tim. Do you?"

The burning sensation on his limbs and the wound to where his ears once were all feel like they are on fire. The pain becomes too much for him to handle and he finally succumbs to the pain.

"All right, fine bitch! Talk! Tell me your fucking story. Get on with it!"

"Okay, a little rude. But I'll forgive you. Now, does the name Jacob Wilson sound familiar?"

Completely uninterested with her question, his response is brimming with sarcasm.

"Should it? I've locked up a lot of scumbags in my career it's possible. So, who was he a friend of yours?"

Suzanne's giddy manner suddenly vanishes, as does her smile; instead she clenches her jaw and looks away before responding to him.

"Yeah, something like that, but you know what's funny you knew him too. I guess I'm going to have to refresh your memory."

Det. Gibson grows frustrated with her vague answers. "Really, so what are we going to do start playing games? Why don't we just play 20 fucking questions?"

She gets up and tosses the chair against the wall. This causes Det. Gibson's eyes to widen in fear as he looks at the raging mad woman she's suddenly become. He watches her as she begins to furiously pace back and forth in front of him.

"No, you know what I got a better idea. Why don't we play, This Is Your Life Detective Gibson?"

Her words bring her smile back after a brief absence due to the joy she got from seeing Det. Gibson almost jump out of his skin. The look of fear on his face fueled her fire once again.

"So Tim, let's go back in time and see if we can refresh your memory.

Suzanne retrieves the chair and places it once again in front of him, resumes her same sitting position before her outburst and begins telling her story to help refresh Det. Gibson's memory.

# CHAPTER 19

"Ten years ago, early in the morning, you went to a home in a very upscale neighborhood to serve an arrest warrant. It was the home of Mr. & Mrs. Jacob Wilson and their two daughters. That day started out like any day in most households in the country. A family was getting up to start the day eating breakfast, the kids then going off to school and the parents either heading off to work or taking care of the household needs.

"This is exactly how the day should have started out for the Wilson family, but unknown to Mr. Wilson; this day would be the beginning of his worst nightmare. An early morning knock on the door started it all…

"Mrs. Wilson said she would answer the door and rushed to open it. Standing in the doorway stood you, Det. Gibson along with three uniformed police officers who stood behind you. You cleared your throat before speaking and said, 'Good morning Mrs. Wilson. Is your husband home? We need to speak with him.'

"At that exact moment, Jacob Wilson, a proud father and husband came down the stairs. He was rolling up the sleeves of his long-sleeved dress shirt, and combed his fingers through his short, chestnut-colored hair that contained some grey on the side around his ears. He asked his wife who was at the door.

"Without giving her a chance to respond to her husband, you pushed your way past Mrs. Wilson and grabbed Mr. Wilson by the collar. You slammed him against the foyer wall and pulled his arms behind his back.

'Mr. Wilson you are under arrest. You have the right to remain silent. Anything you say can and will be used against you in a court of law.' As you recited his Miranda rights, you signaled the uniformed officers to enter.

"One of the policemen stands in front Mrs. Wilson, preventing any possible inference from her during the arrest of her husband. Mr. Wilson didn't resist you at any time during, but he does begin to ask questions about what is he being arrested for.

'What am I being arrested for? You are making a mistake!'

"You ignored Mr. Wilson's questions and continue reading him his rights. He screamed that you were making a huge mistake and asks again what he was being arrested for. He just couldn't understand, why no one would answer his questions. He couldn't comprehend what was happening it felt as if he was in a nightmare that he could not awake from.

"Even though he never resisted, you felt compelled to manhandle him by yanking him off the wall by his collar. You made every attempt him to goad him into doing something giving you the excuse to brutally attack him. Finally, you tell him what he's being arrested for.

'Even though I despise you, you fucking piece of shit, I will tell you. You are being charged with sexual assault, sodomy and child endangerment of your daughter you sick freak!'

"At that moment a female officer can be seen with her arms around his adopted daughter consoling her as she is being escorted out of the house toward a police car. Mr. Wilson sees his daughter being taken out the house and calls out to her.

'Where are you taking her?! Mr. Wilson yelled.

"His concern brings out more disdain from you and you pushed him towards another officer and said, 'Get this piece of shit out of my sight!'"

"During this nightmarish ordeal Mr. Wilson has been completely cooperative, but that comes to an end as it takes both policemen to drag Mr. Wilson out of the house; he struggled as they attempt to drag him out of his home.

"He yelled, 'You are crazy! I would never do anything to hurt my children! Honey, tell them they're making a huge mistake!'

"His mind was racing; confused by everything that was taking place knowing that the only ally he has that will speak up in his defense is his wife. But the moment he looks over at his wife his face turns ashen as he feels his life begin to drain from his body. His wife averted her eyes from him as Det. Gibson places a reassuring hand on her shoulder.

"His head slump and his will to fight left him. As the officers began to walk him toward the door, the sound of running footsteps turned all their attention toward the staircase as an angelic young voice begins to yell out as she runs down the stairs.

'Leave my father alone! He didn't do anything! They're all lying—I heard my mother and sister talking as they made up this story!'

"At the sound of his daughter's voice, Mr. Wilson will to fight is rejuvenated as he used all his strength and pushed the officers, knocking one of them backwards and other off balance. He turned to go toward his young daughter, who had reached the bottom of the staircase running towards him.

"Just as she is about to throw her arms around her father and hug him, you wasted no time placing your arm out to block the young girl and restrained her. The officers each grabbed Mr. Wilson by the arm, this time exerting more pressure on their grip to assure he doesn't get loose again. During this time Mr. Wilson's daughter tries to break free of your grasp, tears rolling down her face.

"Although the officers were instructed to escort Mr. Wilson to a patrol car, their attention is drawn away briefly as they look toward the weeping girl that is being held back by you. Mr. Wilson was completely heartbroken seeing his daughter in her current state. You yell at the officers, 'What are you two waiting for?! Get him out of here!'

"They once again began dragging Mr. Wilson out of his home. Before they get him out to the patrol car Mr. Wilson gave a final glance to his wife. The woman he loved with all his heart, despite her failings, smiled and winked at him.

"Mr. Wilson was taken down to the police station where he was questioned for hours and eventually processed and charged with the rape of his adopted daughter. Mr. Wilson always proclaimed his innocence saying he was framed by you because you were sleeping with his wife, but all his allegations, fell on deaf ears.

"According to the statement given to the police by Mr. Wilson's adopted daughter, she told police that he had raped her during the night. The next morning when Mr. Wilson left for work, she told her mother and she contacted a friend of hers in the police department, which happened to be you. Mrs. Wilson even stated to police that she took her daughter's sheets, underwear and placed them in a bag for police as evidence of what had happened to her.

"When the charges hit the media, nobody came to his defense, the family business that had been around for years went belly up when the news became public and his wife filed her own charges against him claiming years of abuse, both physical and emotional.

"She claimed the reason she didn't speak up sooner was because he threatened that if she came forward he would hurt her. The amount of evidence against Mr. Wilson was overwhelming even though they were lies, his lawyer told him that he may have to consider taking the plea agreement they offered him. One of the conditions of the plea agreement was that he had to admit to sexually assaulting his adopted daughter.

"The second condition is that he would have to register himself as a sexual offender with the state and he would agree not to have any contact with his youngest daughter. Mr. Wilson felt completely trapped; his attorney kept telling him to take the plea deal. So he accepted the plea agreement and he was given four years in prison and upon his release he would be placed on probation for ten years.

"The day after he was sent to prison, he received divorce papers from his wife. Since he had pleaded guilty it made it so much easier for his wife lawyers to rake him over the coals and took everything leaving him penniless. To make matters worse for Mr. Wilson word got around the prison that he was in for molesting his daughter.

"That put a huge red flag on Mr. Wilson back as he was beaten and abused almost daily, even the guards would turn a blind eye to his abuse. Mr. Wilson received a glimmer of hope as he received word from his attorney that he would be released six months early. His glimmer of light and hope was extinguished when later that night they beat him half to death. They beat his face to a bloody pulp, broke his arm in two places and fractured two of his ribs and sexually assaulted him. The viciousness of this attack brought about the attention of the warden and Mr. Wilson's lawyer, so for his safety he was placed in isolation for the remainder of his sentence.

"After spending a horrendous forty-two months in prison, when he was finally released from prison, he fell into a deep depression. Life on the outside was just as bad as life on the inside, everyone he knew distanced themselves from him and three months after he was released, he hung himself."

Suzanne shows a sign of emotion, a small hint of sadness recalling the misery her dad suffered; until some unfortunate words by Det. Gibson bring out the worst in her again.

"Wow, how pathetic such a sad story, if my hands were loose, I would've played the violin for you. You are really fucked up in the head. What does any of this shit have to do with me?"

Suzanne can't believe the words she is hearing as she shakes her head laughing at his idiocy.

"Un-fucking-believable, you just don't get it, do you? You see that's the reason why you lost your ears. You just don't listen."

"Fuck you, you crazy bitch!" He begins yet another round of struggling against his restraints.

Suzanne stands, laughing at his outburst. She leaves the room briefly before re-entering carrying a black duffel bag. Exhausted from his brief exertion, Det. Gibson slumps his head and yells. "What the fuck do you want from me?!"

Ignoring his words and she walks behind him, dropping the bag. He twists his neck frantically, trying to see what she is doing behind him. But no matter how much he struggles he is unable to see anything that she does. She finally returns back to her chair and sits back in front of him, her eyes glowing with anticipation.

"So Det. Gibson, you still don't remember Jacob Wilson? But you do know Deborah Wilson. Oh I'm sorry I mean Deborah Garfield."

The mention of the name causes him to focus on her, as she now has his full attention.

"Deborah?? You leave Deborah out of this."

"Are you fucking kidding me, you jackass? That whore caused all this shit. She helped you frame my father. C'mon, Timmy, You remember my father, he was one of those many scumbags you put in jail."

His eyes widen, as it finally dawns on him, what she has been talking about. He begins to see images; flashbacks of his past actions come rushing back to him. His thoughts seem to overwhelm him as he slumps his head, shaking it from side to side mumbling to himself, feeling that he has been living a nightmare and once he awakens he will be sitting in his car eating his lunch. Suzanne smiles as she watches him, seeing his face go from disbelief to panic.

"OOh...Ooo I think somebody is starting to remember something," Suzanne says with a giggle.

Det. Gibson doesn't look up at Suzanne; he grimaces in pain before speaking in a very soft voice. "Oh, Jesus Christ...I know who you are. You're Deborah's daughter; the one that was admitted into the mental hospital."

Without warning Suzanne pops up from the chair and begins to jump up and down, clapping joyfully. Her actions cause Det. Gibson to jump in fear as he finally looks up at her behavior.

"WOW!!! This is great Mr. Detective finally figured it out. You're not just a pretty face. Well, you use to be a pretty face."

Det. Gibson makes an attempt to defend his actions. "Okay, I know you have been through a lot, but you have to listen to me. I'm really sorry about your father, but you were too young to understand, he was sick man. He raped your sister, he committed a crime. I had to arrest him; I was just doing my job."

Those words cut through Suzanne like a knife. Furious and even more motivated, she marches toward the back of Det. Gibson's chair and pushes it forward causing all the weight of his body to lean into the restraints tearing into his skin.

He screams in agony every time she jerks his body, rage had taken over her and she continued pushing him back and forth, he tries to reason with her hoping it would get her to stop.

"Please, listen! Hurting me isn't going to make things better. Do you know how much trouble you are in right now? If you let me go and I will do everything in my power to get you all the help you need."

She stopped shaking him and walked around to face him; her hands gripped both arm rests and leaned forward her forehead almost touching his.

"Your job! You were just doing your job? Okay, Timmy let's talk about your job."

She backs away from him and paces around the room once again, something she did when she needed some time to breathe and compose herself. She stops suddenly and looks over at him.

"First you frame my father, then you help my mother get me committed and last but not least, you threatened and harassed my father when he got released from prison. Does that about sum up everything about how good a job you did?" She said her stare burning a hole through him.

"Suzanne, I don't know where you got these all these crazy ideas from, but you are completely wrong. I never did anything to frame your father. I had nothing to do with you being admitted into the hospital. I hadn't even seen your father since the trial," he says, hoping that she will believe him.

"Timmy, Timmy, Timmy why do you insist on lying to me? Maybe you need a little refresher."

Suzanne pulls out a small remote control from her jacket pocket points it toward the television and turns it on. The image on the television was of an earlier recording of Dr. Levitt lying on the stretcher moaning in agonizing pain.

"Hey, Tim take a look at the screen. Does the man look familiar?"

Det. Gibson lets out a loud gasp. His reaction brings a smile to her face.

"Okay, I'm not a psychic, but I'm going to take that as a yes, Timmy."

"What are you doing to him?" He asks nervously.

"Nothing that a doctor couldn't fix," Suzanne says as she begins to laugh uncontrollably.

"You sick bitch! You are going to pay for all this, I promise! You will pay!"

"C'mon Timmy, no need to be rude. Even you have to have to admit that was some funny shit. Oh, well let's continue with our story, Mr. Cranky Pants. You are so adamant that you had nothing to do with framing my father, but we all know that's a lie." She says pausing briefly. "We will get back to that later. You also claimed you had nothing to do with having me committed, but unlike you Timmy, Dr. Levitt was a lot more talkative than you."

Det. Gibson couldn't look at her, didn't want to look at her. For the first time, he is becoming more and more terrified of the psychotic woman standing in front of him. He knew anything he said would be considered a lie, so he tried to play the victim and blame Dr. Levitt.

"I don't know what he told you, but that man can't be trusted, he'll say anything to save his ass. He would blame anybody but himself for everything that happened to you. I'm telling you that I didn't do anything to you or your father."

Suzanne pushes a different button on the remote and the image on the television has now changed. The image on the screen is a live feed of Dr. Levitt current condition. The screen reveals a lifeless Dr. Levitt sitting up on his stretcher. His attire is completely drenched in his own blood and his face is unrecognizable as his eye sockets have been hollowed out, there are slithers of loose flesh hanging down from his sockets his face is now pale.

Det. Gibson stares at the image with his mouth hung open. Suzanne was basking in the look of horror and disbelief that is spreading across his face.

"You know what you're probably right about Dr. Levitt. He might have said anything to save his ass, so to make sure that wouldn't happen, I gave him a little shock therapy." She begins shaking, making a mocking gesture of being electrocuted.

Det. Gibson can't believe what he is seeing as he glances up at the image of a bloody Dr. Levitt strapped to that bed.

"You see after his shock therapy sessions, he was a little forthcoming. I believed that he needed more encouragement to open up, so I decided that maybe all Dr. Levitt needed was to see all the harm he had caused everyone."

The corners of her lips curled upward as the more she spoke about this the bigger her smile got as she kept her sights locked on Det. Gibson.

"So I held his left eye open first like this," pulling her own left eye open with her index finger and thumb as she leans into Det. Gibson face..

"I then stuck the scalpel deep into the top part of the eye cutting all the optic nerves. I made sure to move the scalpel around so that I could remove the entire eye intact. When I pulled it out, I was so careful I wanted to make sure that the eye was not damaged. It was some of my best work. I showed him his eye. Let's just say that after that, he was able to see the truth a lot clearer."

Det. Gibson thrashed around in the chair violently trying to get free.

"You are really fucking sick, you know that?! What do you want from me?!"

She switches off the television and takes her seat.

"Timmy, I want to know why. Why did you do it, huh?" She asks in a very soft casual manner.

He bangs the back of his head against the chair head rest feeling completely drained and helpless. He knows that he is trapped and his odds of being released are becoming less with every passing second. At this time his only option is to come clean and tell her the truth his only chance of survival may rest on it. So with his chances of survival resting on his story telling skills he begins his tale.

# CHAPTER 20

"**I** knew your mother for many years; way before she was married. The day she got married, I decided that it would be best if we stopped seeing each other. She told me she was happy and loved her husband very much, but that didn't last too long and in hindsight I wasn't surprised."

He pauses briefly, and looks over at Suzanne, trying to gauge her demeanor to the words that he is saying. But she just stares at him intently not saying a word or showing any emotions, so he continues.

"She reached out to me probably a year after you were born telling me, how bored she was with married life."

For some reason that comment makes Suzanne giggles.

"You know what, I am not surprised. I have been learning so much about dear old mom these past years. Oh, I'm sorry excuse me, I'm being so rude please continue, you know what they say confessions can be wonderful for the soul."

He was tempted to make a quick retort to her comment, but thought better of it and continued with his story.

"One afternoon, she called me at work and told me that your father found out about our affair. She wanted us to meet. So we decided to meet at the Johnston mall's rooftop parking lot. It was there that she showed me an envelope that had come by courier from a private investigator addressed to your father and in the envelope were pictures of your mother and me together.

"By the looks of the places in the pictures, we were being watched for weeks. I told your mother to divorce your father that I would take care of her and both of you girls, but she said if she did she would lose everything. That was the first time, I heard about her plan to pay back your father for spying on her and make sure she would take him for everything he was worth."

Suzanne sat there with a blank stare on her face giving no indication of how all this was making her feel. Det. Gibson was still hoping for some type of reaction to relieve his mind and put him at ease, but unfortunately for him that was not happening. So he carried on telling his story knowing that at the end his fate would be revealed.

"The part of her plan on getting you committed was pretty simple. I had busted a few loan sharks and had their ledgers of people that owed them money. I remember seeing Dr. Levitt in one of those ledgers and the word 'quack' underlined. It turned out Dr. Levitt owed money and was behind on his weekly payment, so I made deal with the loan shark to lose his ledger, if he would forgive Dr. Levitt loan.

"I knew he would do anything to clear his slate, so your mother offered him the money. When he received the money and gave it to the loan shark, as part of our deal the loan shark would return the money back to me. So in reality we got him to sign your commitment papers for free."

Suzanne continues listening as she calmly rises up from the chair and strolls over beside Det. Gibson, as he watches her every move fearing the worst.

She stands beside him, when her foot steps onto the lifting pedal that is underneath his chair and begins pumping it; his body bounces every few seconds with every pump of the pedal as the chair raises a few inches off the ground. This goes on for minutes as the chair is finally lifted about two feet off the ground. Her actions accompanied by her silence make him shout out in fear.

"What are you doing?!"

She doesn't acknowledge his comments as all her movements have now become methodical. Moving slowly with a purpose, she bends down, and unzipping the duffle bag, removes a large section of thick, yellow nylon rope.

Examining the rope briefly before tossing the rope over a large black pipe in the ceiling above Det. Gibson's chair as it lands on the ground on the other side of his chair; she struts over to it and grabs it. Her continued silence along with her current actions causes him to have a complete meltdown.

"Suzanne, please! I told you everything I know! What else do you want from me?!"

She stops, turning toward him, her baby blue eyes glaring at him, before finally acknowledging him as the fear is evident in his face.

"I'm so impressed with you and dear old mom. You guys put together one hell of a plan. You two thought of everything and you both got away with framing an innocent man. The part that I don't understand is why did you continue to harass my father once he was released?"

She waits for answers, but when she receives none she continues.

"You two destroyed him. He was humiliated; disgraced, he lost his family business. That business meant the world to him and a lot of people in the community. The little bit of dignity he had left you decided to take away from him by continuing to harass him. Why?"

He inhaled all his fears and chose to answer; his eyes never make any contact with her as he keeps them focus down on the ground.

"Your mother thought your father was going to try and get you out of the hospital. If that happen then the truth would come out. She wanted to make sure that wouldn't happen, so she asked me to talk to him and tell him to stay away from you. I never thought that he would kill himself."

Suzanne actually believed his words, she knew the words he spoke were genuine, but they still wouldn't help him from receiving a lesson in karma. As she pulls out the rest of the yellow rope from her bag, that section of rope exposes a noose, which she places around Det. Gibson head. That caused the most fight she had seen from him since his imprisonment as she tightened the noose around his chubby neck.

"You see, one of the biggest problems I noticed about you is that you never thought for yourself. Dear old mom would always lead you around by your little head. So let's try an experiment and see what happens when I lead you around by your bigger head," she says, her grin stretching across her face.

She begins picking up the slack of the rope that is lying on the ground beside his chair. The more she pulls on the slack the tighter the noose becomes around his throat; his gurgling noises and the gasping of air become music to her ears. She pulls on it for a few more moments before releasing it; his bright, red face returning back to its normal color minus all the blood streaks around his face. .

She takes the rope and wraps it a few times around the arm chair before finishing it off with one big knot.

"You can't do this! It won't bring back your father!"

"You are right. It won't bring him back, but it will make me feel so warm and cuddly inside." She lets out a morbid laugh.

Det. Gibson writhes violently in the chair, but he stops suddenly, when he realizes the more he starts his ongoing battle with the straps, the tighter the noose is becoming.

"I hope you rot in hell!"

"I've already been there, but if you mention my name, you might get my old room."

She laughs, as she reaches her hand underneath the chair and twist a switch, her leg then extends towards the pedal once again. This time when she pushes down on the pedal the chair begins to lower. Her plan is becoming a reality as the distorted sound of his gurgling is now sounding prominently throughout the room.

Det. Gibson's fingers curled desperately around the chair arm, trying to wiggle his neck out of the death grip it was in trying to mouth some things the words are incoherent until he shouts out his final words.

"I'm... I'm sorry, I...I... didn't mean those things... I'm so sorry!"

His face shifts from a rose petal red to a deep bruised purple as Suzanne admires her work caressing his face.

She leans into his face seeing up close the damage the thick rope is doing by digging into his skin. She places both her hands on each side of his face kisses his forehead and says a few final words to the man who didn't give her the chance to reunite with her father.

"Tim, I know you're sorry. I can hear it in your voice. I see it in your face. Too bad, I don't give a fuck remember? I'm a crazy, sick bitch."

Her hands slide off his sweaty face and she exits the room, closing the door behind her as she with glee, skips down the abandoned hall, cackling as she hears a halfhearted gurgling scream coming from his room.

# CHAPTER 21

Throughout this entire ordeal, Deborah finds herself still refusing to believe the reality that is around her. She continues to contemplate different ways to remove the cast iron shackle from around her wounded ankle.

Each time her bony fingers slid underneath it in an extreme effort to slip it off, she wails out in excruciating pain. Her ankle, at this point, was severely swollen with pieces of her skin, along with dry blood attached to the shackle.

She coughed every now and again, her throat dry and irritated needing to be rehydrated. Her mind begins to ponder several scenarios; maybe this faceless stranger wanted her to die in this room. Her mind cuts off the instant she hears that familiar sound of the small door sliding open.

Her mouth reflexively began to salivate and the thought of food touching the inner corners of her lips drove her eyes to focus on the entrance.

On this occasion there was only one silver bowl and a silver plate tossed into her room, this time; the contents in the plate were more satisfactory. A sandwich sat on top of the plate and water occupied the bowl they were gently slid into the room and the small door slammed shut.

Deborah slides off the bed gingerly, the pain becoming unbearable, but finds herself crawling toward the food quickly. She snatches the sandwich off the plate almost swallowing it whole at times even choking from her hastened pace, not taking the time to savor each bite or concern when she would receive her next meal.

She reaches out for the water bowl gulping it down quickly in between bites, which causes her to choke even more from the combination of chewing on the sandwich and gulping down the water.

As she sits their coughing trying to clear her airway, the steel door swings open and in enters her hooded captor, standing in front of her staring down at her.

"You should take smaller bites. I wouldn't want you to choke prematurely."

Deborah is startled that the voice beneath the mask and hood belongs to a female. She then tosses the left over piece of sandwich on the plate, weakly pushing both the plate and bowl away from her. She glares up at her masked captor defiantly.

"I want to know where my daughter is! What have you done to her?"

The hooded figure taps an index finger on the side of her head, mocking the gesture of someone trying to recall something.

"Damn… Now where did I put that girl? Let me see the last time I saw her; she was giving me a very severe tongue lashing. She was so serious, but we will talk more about her later. Let's talk about you, how you doing?" She inquires with a burst of laughter.

The more the masked marauder laughs at her expense the angrier it is making Deborah, so she reverts again to something that has helped her before get her out of trouble.

"What do you want? Is it money? I have lots of money. Tell me how much and I can get it for you!"

"The first time you offered me money I told you money wouldn't help you or your daughter, but here you are again offering it again. You just don't get that money is not going to help you. That seems to always be your answer to everything. Throw money in front of it and hope it will go away. Isn't that how you solved your problem ten years ago?"

Deborah's anger ceases as the reality of that statement causes her to think carefully about her response.

"I have no idea, what you are talking about."

The figure takes a step closer toward Deborah who slides herself back toward the bed, her back pressing against the cold metal bed frame.

"I know all about you, Deborah. I think it's about time that we should bond. Don't you think that would be a great idea? Mom?"

With those shocking words being said, the captor slowly lowers the hood off her head and snaps off the mask dropping it on the floor, revealing her identity. Deborah's face looks like all the blood has drain from it as she stares at the familiar face. This was the one day she thought would never happen as the truth came crashing painfully in front of her.

"Suzanne! No, no, it can't be…"

Deborah gradually recoils her legs into her chest and her head slumps into her blood stained knees rocking back and forth, feeling the violent whirlwinds of the reality now facing her. "This has to be a dream, a real bad dream. When I open my eyes, all this will be just a bad dream." She mumbles to herself, crying into her legs.

Suzanne takes this time, while Deborah is in a state of disarray as a cue for her to exit the room briefly, re-entering with a chair and a small leather pouch. She positions the chair underneath the TV and drops the leather pouch next to her chair.

"Why? Why? This is all just a bad dream... really why don't you give it a rest?" she says, mocking her mother's words and sobs. "Can you freaking be any more dramatic? After all the pain you caused everyone, do you really need to ask why?"

Deborah attempts to rise up and sit on the bed, but she lacks the strength and falls back to the ground trying to speak through all her sobs. "I always did my best to try and be a good mother. You don't understand, you needed help after your father was arrested. You were saying some of the craziest things and acting out. I was so afraid you would hurt yourself."

Suzanne is trying her best to hold her composure and refrain from showing any emotions. But she realizes she can't hold it anymore and goes into a frenzy of unstoppable laughter.

"You are so fucking hilarious! You were trying to be a good mother that is biggest oxymoron I have ever heard. You are the reason that my father was arrested, not just you there also was the help you got from my beautiful sister Ariel. C'mon mom, don't you remember?"

Suzanne stands and removes her black robe dropping it straight to the ground. Underneath the robe she is still wearing her blue zip up jacket, red t-shirt, black jeans and blood-stained sneakers. Returning to her seat her eyes fixate on her mother with complete disdain as she begins to refresh her mother's memory.

"Okay mommy, as I have said before if one wants to understand something the best way to do it is always start from the beginning. Ten years ago, you walked into Ariel's room right after my dad went to work. You wanted to speak privately with her, thinking I was still asleep and no one would be able to hear you. Unbeknownst to you, I was sitting outside on the balcony outside her open window. You were really upset about something that morning. I heard everything you said, everything you both planned."

# CHAPTER 22

"Ariel was lying comfortably on her bed, her headphones plugged into her ears. The room had every kind of luxury you would expect in a room that belonged to a prima donna. Ariel always made sure her room had the best and newest items, her desk had a brand new laptop computer, a 42" television, a closet full of the swankiest clothes and the shoes to match.

"You entered her room and walked over to her, waving your hands in front of her face to get her attention, as her music was blasting into her ears. You yanked off one of her headphones and Ariel stared angrily up at you.

'Don't you know how to knock?' She asked.

"You told her to drop the attitude and to fucking listen. Ariel rolled her eyes before taking off the other headphone. You were pacing nervously around Ariel's spacious room. I was able to peer through the curtains. I wanted to make sure I heard every word you both said carefully. You told her that her father had found out about Tim. How he'd hired a private investigator to follow you and had pictures. Ariel then said, first, he wasn't her father and second she warned you to be careful, that he wasn't a stupid as he looked.

"You said, 'Well that's not going to fucking help me now! Once he sees those photos, he is going to file for divorce. We will have nothing.'

"You then stop talking and took a seat beside her on the bed. You told her you had an idea on how to fix it so that you didn't lose everything but you needed her help. You informed her that if she went along with your plan and did everything you said, you both could get all of his money and property.

"I could not believe the words that were coming out of your mouth, I felt as if someone had punch me in the pit of my stomach. But what I saw next made me feel even more disgusted and angry as you patted Ariel's knee a big wide smile came across Ariel's face. She excitedly jumped out of bed.

'Really, are you kidding me? Sign me up! What do I have to do?' she said.

"I could not believe what I was seeing and hearing, my so-called sister and mother planning against my father. You told her all she had to do was like he was coming on to her and acting inappropriately. To act as if she was afraid to say anything about one night when he came into her room and forced her to have sex with him.

"I was stunned at how easy the words nonchalantly flowed out your mouth. When you finished talking Ariel seemed hesitant. I thought that maybe for a minute she was growing a conscience. But no, she only questioned whether the authorities would examine her to find any evidence of them having sex. You informed her that you would seduce him and collect some of his semen. Ariel listen intently nodding in approval as you continued laying out every detail of your diabolical plan.

"You said in the morning you would plant the evidence in her sheets and panties. Then you would call Tim who would take care of his part. The main thing you were concerned with was Ariel putting on a convincing performance to the police about being raped.

"I didn't know how much more of this I could take, I felt like charging from the balcony and attacking you both. I sat there with tears flowing down my face as I could not believe the heartless way you both were planning on destroying my father's life.

"Then Ariel suddenly begins her practice performance, feigning despair as she spoke.

'He came into my room. I told him to get out but he wouldn't leave. He got on top of me, put his right hand over my mouth and ripped my panties off with his free hand. He was so strong..I..I...I couldn't fight him off. I tried to scream but he told me he'd hurt me if I did. I just wanted it to be over, so I closed my eyes until he was done. When he finished, he got off me and told me this would be our secret. I felt so dirty. I didn't know what to do so I took off my night gown and bed sheets and placed them in the hamper.' She then broke into fake sobs. In an instant she spoke back in her normal voice and said, 'Please, no autographs.'

'Holy crap, that was pretty impressive. You had me fooled, I thought for a minute he really raped you," you said.

"You and Ariel hugged one another and laughed before discussing additional details of your evil and twisted plan. I got up and quietly entered the door to my room. I fell onto my bed and bawled my eyes out. My first thought was trying to figure a way to warn my father of what I just overheard. How could I convince him....?"

Suzanne leans forward in the chair and stares at Deborah, her eyes fixated on to hers.

"I'm pretty sure you remember that night as clearly as I do, I tried to tell my father as soon as he came home from work. I don't know if you had a slight inkling that I may have overheard something but you did everything within your power to keep him away. You kept him busy eventually telling him you had made dinner reservation and got him out the house. He promised to speak to me when he got home. I tried to stay up, but fell asleep. Of course, when I awoke that fateful morning… I don't need to go further as you know the rest."

Suzanne never blinked, as she spoke with deliberation to her mother, every word was a remainder of the hell that her father and her endured at the hands of the person who was supposed to show her unconditional love.

Deborah rolled her eyes and sucked her teeth at the story Suzanne has just told. "You don't know what you are talking about."

Suzanne shakes her head smiling. "I know more than you think mother. See, I had someone helping me fill in the blanks."

Her words bring about a sudden interest in Deborah as her eyes widen with curiosity.

"And who would that be?"

"Well to be honest, there were really two people who helped me."

Deborah's short lived curiosity reverts to unadulterated rage. "You are so full of shit! That's the reason you ended up in the hospital—because of that crazy imagination!"

Suzanne smiles at Deborah reaches inside her jacket and pulls out a leather spiral bound book. Deborah's ire dwindles when her eyes come into contact with the book.

"You see mother, my father kept a journal about everything from the moment he learned of your affair, his time in prison, life after prison. The last entry in his book was the day he killed himself. He left the journal and the location of a large sum of money he was saving for me with a friend of his named Michael."

Suzanne flips through the pages of the book as Deborah sits, now speechless.

"You see, that friend helped me get out of that place that resembled a hospital and gave me everything my father left for me. Since my release I have read through all the documents he left for me and for the last three years I have been watching you all. Learning everything about you fuckers and today is redemption day."

"Um...I." Deborah has no words for the first time; she has no quick retorts as Suzanne tucks the book back into her jacket. Deborah seems to be in some sort of trance, until a loud clap echoing throughout the room snaps Deborah out of her trance.

"Holy crap, let's hear it world! The woman is finally speechless."

Suzanne stands and walks around the room. Deborah's eyes follow her every move unsure of what will happen next.

"You see mom...I'm sorry. May I call you mom? You kept my commitment a secret. My father had no idea what happened to me after he was sent to jail. When his friend Michael visited him in jail, he asked him to find me. Once my father was released, Michael had him move in and that was when he found out where I was. He wanted to reach out to me to get me out, but you made sure that could never happen."

Suzanne inches closer to Deborah with every step, her anxiety and fear levels grows.

"The court gave you full custody; you took it a step further and took out a restraining order against him making sure he couldn't come within 1000 feet of me."

The tips of Suzanne's blood stained sneakers were lightly brushing up against Deborah's bruised legs as she loomed over her.

"Even after all the pain you caused him, you were still not satisfied. You kept pushing and pushing until he fell into a deep depression. He tried to contact you so many times, tried to get you to release me, but instead of you talking to him, you took it a step further and released your pet detective on him."

Deborah was twitching uncontrollably, looking from side to side, her body wrought with anxiety.

"My father wrote in his journal about the night that would eventually be his last. My dad was leaving the grocery store and your pet dick Timmy approached him on the street. He stopped him, frisked him, and threatened to kill him if he didn't stay away from you."

Not one muscle from Deborah's body moved as Suzanne kept her intimidating stance in front of her.

"The journal spoke of many nights where Det. Gibson would harass him, it started the day he was released up to the day he gave up and killed himself. My father was good to you and your daughter. He didn't deserve what you did to him."

A tear rolls down her face and Suzanne spins around quickly to wipe her cheek, angry at herself for showing that type of emotion now.

Deborah's rage returns and again as she begins another rant. "Don't you talk to me about what he did or didn't deserve! What about what I deserved? He was going to divorce me and leave me with nothing! Nothing!"

Deborah's outburst gives her the strength to pull herself up to the floor. She sits on the bed and seethes with anger. Suzanne overlooks her outburst and unnoticed by Deborah, pulls out her remote from her pocket turning on the television. The screen showed no image just a grayish static that illuminates the room making it slightly brighter. No words are spoken by Suzanne just a deathly scowl until she finally breaks her silence.

"Are you fucking for real bitch?! You took care of him? Really? You gave him a daughter—oh I feel the love! You made his life worthwhile by fucking another man and making him look like a fool!"

Suzanne digs deep into her jean pocket and pulls out a crumpled piece of paper. She tosses it in Deborah's face, hitting her square between the eyes. Deborah glares up at her before picking up the crumbled up paper and opening it.

The paper is a photo a very revealing snap shot of Deborah and Det. Gibson during one of their afternoon liaisons at some hotel. She dropped the photo and let out a scream in frustration. She felt completely helpless. She thought Tim had gotten rid of all the photos.

"You are all responsible for what happened to him. In life, there are consequences for the decision and actions you do." She said.

Suzanne clicks the remote again and the screen is now playing video footage of Ariel, carrying a few shopping bags as she strolls out of the mall.

"Where's my daughter?!"

Suzanne smirks at her sudden burst of energy as she rises off the bed.

"Ah, yes your daughter. A chip off the old block huh mom? Shopping like you, always spending the money that was taken from a man she claimed was not her father."

Suzanne clicks on the remote again changing the video feed; this one is a recording of Ariel trapped in her holding cell, barely able to move the straps restricting her movements. Deborah whispers her name, not able to control her tears as they flow uncontrollably down her face.

"What have you done to her?" she asked, her voice cracking with every word.

"Who me, I'm insulted? I haven't done anything. She did this to herself. Remember, there are no victims here. Even me; I no longer consider myself a victim. I'm a survivor. Unlike some other people you might know."

Suzanne clicks the remote once more and this time it's a live feed of Ariel.

She is completely motionless blood dripping slowly from her scalp and her mouth down the front of her blouse, around the chair and the floor

Deborah gasps and lunges toward Suzanne in an uncontrollable rage, but collapses to the ground, her weakened legs unable to withstand the sudden pressure. She lies face down on the ground sobbing and pounding her hands onto the concrete floor.

"No! You horrible bitch! You've killed her!"

Suzanne squats down beside her and pats her dirty mangled hair.

"Awwwwww... You look so sad, mommy. Don't be sad, she did have some final words for you. I think they were 'NO! Stop! Please!' something like that. It was kind of hard for me to understand her without this."

Suzanne stands up, walks over to the chair, and retrieves the black pouch from under it. She takes a seat and places the pouch on her lap. Deborah's eyes are completely blood shot as she finally looks up, feeling completely numb inside, her tears obscuring her vision as she tries to focus on what Suzanne has on her lap.

Seeing that she is focused on the pouch, Suzanne tosses it to her and it lands near her on the floor. She backs away from the pouch, fearing what might be in it.

"Open it! Open it! It's something that will remind you of Ariel I promise." Suzanne says beaming and clapping her hands like an excited child on Christmas.

Deborah reaches out, feeling around for the pouch while keeping a cautious eye on Suzanne who still has that huge smile on her face. She finally grabs the pouch placing it on her lap never turning her eyes away from Suzanne as she unzips the pouch. When she opens the pouch far enough to peer inside, her eyes catch a glimpse of something so horrific that she screams and tosses the pouch away placing her hands over her face.

Suzanne stands and reaches for the pouch, then returns to her seat. She reaches inside the pouch and pulls out a human tongue, doused in blood placing next to the right side of the chair.

"You see I told you it would be something that would remind you her. Your daughter loved to talk but she just didn't know how to tell the truth. So now she will never have to worry about telling a lie or for that matter say anything forever.

Deborah sits up squeezes the top of her stomach and smacks her clammy hand over her chapped lips, feeling queasy she begins to cough. That is all it takes for chunks of food and bile to pour out of her mouth and nose splashing unto the floor. The stench of her puke filling the room.

"How could you? She was your sister!" She says struggling with the words, while wiping the remains of the puke from her mouth. On the other hand Suzanne seems to be enjoying the sight of her mother current condition. Deborah scoots backward away from pile of barf that is near her; as Suzanne twirls the pouch around in her right hand.

Suzanne points the remote up at the monitor with her left hand clicking on it changing it back to its grayish static state. She places the pouch on her lap watching Deborah sob uncontrollably. She tries using the bed to pick herself off the floor, but in her current disoriented and lethargic nature her body just slides back to the ground.

"I'm sorry. I'm so sorry. I wish I could take it all back. Please forgive me. I'm sorry." She begged.

Without saying a word Suzanne clicks the remote now showing a video feed of Dr. Levitt, tossing and squirming while strapped to the stretcher.

"Do you remember good old Dr. Levitt? The man you paid to have me committed? The man, who watched me get abused, tortured and rape during my stay at the hospital?"

Deborah looks up to the screen recognizing Dr. Levitt, unable to say anything she just stares at his image. Suzanne takes her silence as an opportunity to keep switching the video feeds, so that she can enjoy the beautiful image of Dr. Levitt before and after.

The new live video feed shows Dr. Levitt sitting in his own blood, lifeless and eyeless. Deborah painfully bawls; her voice just a coarse breath as she hides her face in her hands, not being able to look at the image any longer.

Suzanne wasn't sure if Deborah had seen that other special something that was in the pouch, so Suzanne re-opens the pouch and pulls out two eyes. She smiles down at them reminiscing on the skill it took to gain these into her possession. She holds both of them up playfully near her eyes, making sure the pupils were directly looking toward Deborah.

"Hey, mom did you know people all say that the eyes are the windows into your soul, but when I look into these two, I don't see anything. Oh well." She says nonchalantly as she tosses them over her shoulder onto the floor behind her

A heart-stopping scream escapes from Deborah's mouth and she squints up at Suzanne, terrified beyond belief quivering uncontrollably.

"Why are you doing this?"

"Really, you can't be that stupid, you just don't get it. You're asking me, when you should be asking yourself that question. You destroyed my father's life along with Ariel's, Dr. Levitt's and of course the love of your life, Timmy."

Suzanne stands and clicks on her remote once again, changing the feed from Dr. Levitt to someone Deborah knew very well. Det. Gibson was sitting in the chair, blindfolded struggling just like everyone else all sadly believing they would escape.

"Suzanne, my god he is a cop! He is a good man. Have you lost your mind?!"

Suzanne bends over and slaps her thigh, cackling at her question. "Have I lost my mind? Helloooooo look around you bitch. What do you think? I'm way beyond losing my mind. I'm reborn. I'm liberated."

Deborah looked at her, planning her next words carefully. Suddenly her head starts throbbing and she feels lightheaded and starts rubbing her forehead.

Suzanne noticed what is happening and looks down at her ill mother.

"Are you okay mommy? Feeling a little dizzy? Maybe you shouldn't have eaten so fast." Deborah glances over at the bowl of water and the plate that was still holding a piece of her leftover sandwich.

"So this is what it all boils down to? You just wanted to bring me here to poison me? Kill me? Why didn't you just kill me? Why did you wait so long? Will killing me make you feel good?!"

"Poison you? Why would I do that to you? You're my mommy. You are so judgmental. You're just like Detective Timmy," she say, pointing up at the monitor.

"He thought I was going to kill him too, but that was so untrue. I just wanted him to feel how my father felt," she said.

With the click of a button on Suzanne's trusty old remote it changed the image now showing a live video feed of Det. Gibson's current state hanging from the thick rope that had appeared almost to have dissolved into his throat as his body dangled between the rope from the ceiling and his restraints holding him down in his chair.

His eyes had remained opened; the side of his head showed the work Suzanne had done earlier a bloody hole where his ear used to me bits of cartilage hanging from his bloody, swollen ear canal.

Deborah bottom lip quivers as she cups her hand over her mouth, not believing that the man she loved was dead.

"You killed him! You killed Tim! He was a good man!"

Deborah makes another attempt on reaching the bed, but falls once again as her vision becomes blurring with every passing moment.

"What did you do to me?" Deborah asks.

Suzanne kneels down leaning closer to her, meeting her eyes intently.

"You destroyed my childhood and you took away my father, but you could never take away the memories

I have of him. The reason you are here in this place is because to find closure in a person's life they must go back to the beginning. I have brought you to this place because this is what was built by my father's family. What you did not only destroyed his family name, but hurt many other families; people lost their jobs because of what you did to my father. My father loved you, he met you here."

Suzanne notices that her mother is starting to go unconscious. She gives her mother a quick smack across the face making sure to keep her conscious just a little bit longer.

"Don't pass out yet. I have one final thing to say. I want you to understand that when you awaken there will be a last meal served. But you might not like the main course. Goodbye mommy, Love you."

Suzanne slides her mother hair away from face and gives her one last parting gift, holding her head with two hands; she gently kisses her forehead and the releases her head as she blacks out.

# CHAPTER 23

Deborah is stirring around on the floor, her back and side feeling the pain of sleeping on the hard concrete floor. When she finally awakens her eyes try to focus on her surroundings. Her head is throbbing from whatever caused her to pass out. She hears a low buzzing sound in the room; looks up and sees the television is still on, showing no images just a gray static snow.

She stretches her limbs feeling the pain from her knee. Gently moving her ankle, squeezing her eyes anticipating the pain she knew would shoot up her leg, when she realizes it's not restricted.

She sat up quickly and look's down at her bare ankle; severely bruised and bleeding no longer shackled. She rubs her eyes making sure they're are not playing tricks on her. The shackle is gone, the chain is gone and the only things that can be seen are the blood stains on the ground from her ankle. She pulls her leg up cautiously to exam her swollen ankle closely, when she realizes the door is ajar. The promise that she might be able to get away fills her heart with hope.

Even though the door is ajar the thought of Suzanne running in goes through her mind. She is unable to run and too weak to defend herself. Now that she can move freely, she rises using the wall and the bed as a crutch, once she is up she limps with caution toward the door.

Her head is still throbbing, but doesn't care, it is now or never. This might be her only opportunity to escape; she approaches the doorway and opens the door. Even though she feels apprehensive she pokes her head out looking down the hallway hoping to see a glint of the outside world. She sees nothing in the utter darkness that resembles a dark hole. But she knows she must walk through it to reach freedom. She drags her weak ankle across the ground using the wall for support limping slowly staying focused and determine to get away from her hell.

A few minutes of walking down this eerie dark passage, she notices a thin line of light peering through the bottom of what appears to be door at the end of the hallway. It was bright enough to give her the indication of daylight, calling out to her from the other side of that door.

She attempts to quicken her pace even though the pain of her ankle limits her speed, her heart races at the sheer hope of life on the other side. A loud crash freezes her in her tracks; she holds her breath as she scans around behind her trying to see anything moving in the darkness. Not hearing any further sound, she continues limping along when she trips on an unknown object that causes her face to slam against the concrete floor; the impact splits her lip and loosens a tooth sending blood from her mouth.

While she cries in severe agony, she gets back up using the wall for support. Though her face and mouth have now joined her ankle in pain, with determination she moves forward. Focused on that glint of light ahead of her, suddenly an illumination engulfs her from behind.

She turns and sees a large television hanging down from the ceiling something she never saw in the darkness. The image on the screen is completely white it has lit up the entire hallway. Deborah's heart jumps into her throat anticipating that Suzanne was going to reappear and drag her back into her room.

Suddenly, the white screen dissipates and Suzanne's face appears on the screen with a wide, impish grin stretched from ear to ear.

"Well mom, by now as you're limping your way down the hallway you must be wondering to yourself, why I let you go." She said, cheerfully.

Suzanne gleeful demeanor infuriates Deborah.

"You just wait! I'm going to tell them every fucking thing you did! I'm going to make sure you pay for all of this and go to prison—just like your daddy!"

Feeling her freedom was near, Deborah laughs out loud.

"The reason I let you go is simple. Ten years ago you did something that hurt my father, me and many other people. But you also hurt someone that was very close to me. I found out that instead of getting rid of my dog, you took it a step further like always and kept him tied up and starved him. Before you took your nap, I told you that there was going to be a last meal served today. Unfortunately for you, the main course is you."

In the blink of an eye, the television turns off immersing the hallway once again in complete darkness, leaving Deborah completely confused. A feeling of paranoia comes over her as her eyes dart from side to side, fearing Suzanne would attack her any second.

She finally decides not to stand still and wait for Suzanne to attack her. Even with the throbbing pain throughout her body, she begins limping quickly, toward the light and freedom. After moving forward a few steps, she hears something in the darkness ahead. She stops and listens, trying to identify the noise. The pitter-pattering sound keeps getting louder as it appears it is coming closer to her.

Slowly she begins to back up, when she see two pairs of eyes moving slowly forward completely in sync with the sound. It finally dawns on her what the sound is and what it belongs to. The growling sound gets louder and she recalls that sound every time Suzanne dog would look at her.

"Oh, God no! She wouldn't!" Deborah screamed. She turns, attempting to run in the opposite direction. "Suzanne what have you done?!"

when two large black and brown German Shepherds, the same type of dog that Suzanne loved and raised begin their charge hungrily toward her, their teeth curling over their lips; their eyes set on their next feast.

Deborah sees the open door to her room; what was before her prison she now hopes will be her salvation. Suddenly the door slams shut automatically, she bangs viciously on the door until her hands become bloody, but it's too late. The dogs are on top of her; two large black and brown German Shepherds, the same breed of dog as the one Suzanne loved so much. Their weight is unbearable on top of her already injured leg and this causes her to topple over as they mount her in a vicious manner. Their teeth curled over their lips; their eyes on their next feast.

She brings up her hands trying to protect her face from one dog, as the other bites into the open wound of her already injured knee and ankle. Her screams accompanied by the sound of their growls, while they chew on her flesh echoes throughout the darken hallway. Weakly, she tries to fight them off as they bite into her hands savagely attack her, their weight keep her pinned to the ground and she has no strength to get them off of her.

"Suzanne! Please help me! I'm your mother!"

Those would be Deborah's last words as her attempts to protect her face finally falter and the dog break through her weaken grip, biting deep into her throat causing a gasp as the last bit of air leaves her lungs. The only sound remaining is that coming from the dogs chewing her flesh.

Suzanne switches off  monitor number seven, the one she had saved just for this moment as she rises from her seat, smiling. She walks out of the control room and saunters up towards the door Deborah so desperately was trying to reach the door that would have led to her freedom. As Suzanne opens the door the bright light of the rising sun warms her face, she takes a few steps outside and looks around the mill, the place that her father had cherished and he had hoped he could one day pass down to her.

She looks up to the sky admiring the beautiful colors this morning, she then raises two fingers, brings them to her lips kiss them and lifts them up to the sky, pointing up toward a wide, puffy clouds.

"I told you dad that I would get them all. That I would make them all pay. I love you, Dad. I just have a little more unfinished business," she says, as she winks, puts her hands into her jacket pockets and walks off.

# EPILOG☒ E

It's a dark, chilly night as the flags outside Tremont Mental Institution flap wildly in the wind. The weather along with the obscurity of the night gives the institution a gloomy feel.

The night shift at the institution normally operates with a very small staff, so when she walks into the lobby, it's not a surprise to find it empty except for the lone receptionist. She appears to be very frustrated with her caller. She raises a finger in her direction signaling to her that she will be with her soon. She stands waiting patiently in front of the receptionist's desk, as the receptionist raises her voice with her caller.

"Yes, I understand Madam, but Doctor Levitt is not available. I can transfer you to Dr. Thomas's voice mail; he is currently handling all of Dr. Levitt's patients."

The receptionist pauses and looks in her direction rolling her eyes, pointing to the phone. She smiles back at the receptionist waiting patiently as her eyes wander around the waiting room. White walls, ugly painting on the wall and not much else, the place really hasn't changed in all these years.

"Madam, I understand what you are saying, but I just don't know when Dr. Levitt will be in to work. All I can do is transfer you to Dr. Thomas's line. Please hold," she said, hanging up the phone, sighing before signaling her that she is ready to help her.

"I'm so sorry for the delay. Some people are just so stubborn. How can I help you?"

"Yes, hello, my name is Judith Silver. I'm the temporary nurse's aide. The agency told me that I start tonight."

She handed over her paperwork and watched as the receptionist browsed over them. After a few seconds, she picks up the phone and to connect with the paging system.

"Steve, report to the front desk. Steve, please report to the front desk." She hangs up the phone and smiles warmly at her. "It will be a minute, please have a seat."

About five minutes, in walks an overweight man with grayish hair on the sides of his scalp. He is unshaven, wearing white hospital scrubs that appear more grey than white. He walks up to the desk, irritated and snaps at the receptionist.

"Yeah what do you want?"

Unbothered by his behavior, she points over to her. "That is Judith Silver, the temp overnight nurse's aide. She starts tonight."

Steve turns and looks her over like a hungry man looking at a steak dinner, smiling while exposing his yellowish, brown teeth. She stares at him with disgust and hatred as images flash through her head. He doesn't recognize her, but her disguise of a red wig and square rim glasses help give her a new appearance. Even without the wig and glasses, she doesn't believe that she would have been recognized, but she didn't want to take the chance of anything ruining her plans.

She stands and smiles back, keeping her emotions in control.

"Hi, nice to meet you," she says with a smile.

She extends her hand to him, he touches it and she feels every part of her body cringe with repulsion. He shakes her hand with his right, but then reaches out with his left, placing it on top.

She feels both of his greasy, calloused dirty hands on hers. The thought of pushing the bridge of his nose into his brain brings a diminutive grin to her face. This makes it so much easier to handle him touching her hands.

"Well, hello it must be my lucky day. Don't you worry you are in good hands. I will teach you everything you need to know," he said.

She smiles back at him patting his hands, the images of him dying slowly keeps her spirits up.

"That's good to know. By the way, I heard the receptionist say Dr. Levitt is not in? He was a family friend and I wanted to say hi." She had to keep herself from bursting into laughter.

Appearing to be bothered that the focus is not on him causes him to become very dismissive. "Yeah, who the hell knows? These doctors do whatever they want thinking they're gods. He left the hospital after work one night about a month ago and no one has seen him since. The police have been looking for him, with no luck," Steve replies while ogling her body.

"Wow that is so weird. Maybe he just needed some time off. He is probably just sitting back in some secluded place enjoying the scenery and taking it easy," she replied, as a small grin appeared on her face.

Steve walks over to the doors, leading her into the ward.

"Who cares about the doc, let's get back to you. I will be in charge of your training, so that means you have to do everything I say. I hope you don't have trouble following instructions."

"Don't worry, I'm a fast learner. You never know I might end up showing you a thing or too." She gave him a wink.

The flirtatiousness of her comment causes a blush to touch Steve's cheeks.

"Um…Okay, well let me show you around." Steve begins his tour taking her down the same hallways that she had been dragged through so many years ago. The memories start to rush back as Steve stops in front of two doors, each one with a small sliding door at the bottom for food to be delivered.

"These rooms are for our special cases," he said.

Steve steps in front of a door marked 1A and bangs on it, it confuses her briefly until the door opens. A tall thin man with long black stringy pony tail, a small scruffy goatee and stained yellow teeth walks out tying up his scrub pants.

It was John, the other goon from her past. She tried to peek into the room through the slightly open door. She was unable to see in, but the crying and whimpering coming from inside the room confirmed the thoughts that went through her mind that some things never change.

She stared at John's face, thinking of all the times he would slip into her room late at night. Her anger boils under her skin. The only way she knows to relieve her anger is to fantasize about different ways to torture them. So the thought of how nice it would be to hang

John by his pony tail until the top of his scalp would rip off made her feel warm all over.

All of a sudden, the sound of their obnoxious voices jolts her back into reality. "Hey, what's with the interruption? I was in the middle of a counseling session," he said, as they both burst into laughter. The familiarity of the moment sends a chill up her spine.

"Yeah I bet," Steve said.

John looks over at her and stares for a few seconds. She looks to the ground hoping he doesn't recognize her. John finally breaks the awkward silence.

"Who's this?" John asks.

Steve looks over at John and smiles. Oh yeah this is Judith Silver, our temp overnight nurse's aide."

John walks over to her and sticks out his pale, white hand. When she extends hers, he grabs it firmly and starts to rub the back of her hand with his thumb, keeping his eyes locked on her. She notices that his hand has some fresh red scratch marks on the top; she is sure it's from the victim he had just left.

"Welcome to the night shift, darling."

He notices her eyes on his scratches and nonchalantly makes light of them

"Sorry about the scratches. Sometimes these patients get a little frisky, but overall don't worry, you are in good hands," he stated.

John glances over at Steve and they both stare at her. She is sure they are contemplating some elaborate plan to get her alone. She returns their smiles as she takes her hand back from John's creepy grip, but John keeps looking at her.

"I'm curious. Have you been a nursing aide for long? You do look kind of familiar."

She puts her head down and turns her body slowly away from him, trying to act shy and inconspicuous.

"Well to be honest, I haven't been a nurse's aide for long. My main job is party planning."

"That's good to know. Because what a coincidence, we love to party. Right, John?" Steve said, slyly elbowing John.

"Awesome, I'm currently planning a private party for some important clients," she said.

This gets their attention and whatever curiosity John might have had about her vanishes.

"Normally, these parties are for the clients and the guests they invite only, but since we are going to be working together, it might be cool to get to know each other outside of work. Every party is different so there might be some drinks, some food, some dancing and sometimes some unexpected surprises," she said, excitedly awaiting their response.

Steve is so flustered and excited; he jumps almost out of his skin to accept the invitation before John can even get his mouth open.

"Sure we'd love to. We promise we will behave." The duo laughs in harmony.

"Don't behave too much. It is a party. These are the kinds of parties, where anything can happen."

"Okay it sounds fucking awesome. Maybe I will have the chance to experience some of those surprises with you," he said, enthusiastically.

She walks over to Steve and John, a devious smile playing on her lips thinking of all the wonderful things she has in store for them.

"Sounds like a plan boys. I will definitely make sure that there will be some unexpected surprises for each of you. You can just imagine the fun; we are going to have a blast! The last party I hosted had so many surprises that it still brings a smile to my face."